SO MANY HEISTS, SO LITTLE TIME . . .

THIEVES' DOZEN

Horse Laugh: Dortmunder always avoids thefts that involve four-legged creatures. Then why is he somewhere out in New Jersey, listening to sirens wailing in the distance, holding on for dear life to a runaway racehorse's rear end?

Too Many Crooks: Dortmunder plans for everything. But when he started digging a tunnel under a bank, the one thing he didn't think of was coming out a hero . . .

Party Animal: Desperate? On the run? Chased by the police with a handful of loot? For every emergency, Dortmunder has an answer. This time it's slipping into a party and helping a comely caterer serve anchovy logs—until the cops come in . . .

Now What?: There's a guy riding the New York subway with a ham sandwich in a paper bag. The guy's name is Dortmunder and the sandwich has a $300,000 brooch inside. It all started at a celebrity wedding party in Manhattan . . .

Art and Craft: Nothing good had ever come from dealing with a crook named Three Finger Gillie. Now that Gillie has turned into a downtown artist, it's even worse. He wants Dortmunder to steal his own paintings—and Dortmunder just knows that something's wrong . . .

Please turn this page for acclaim for Donald E. Westlake . . .

D0052714

PRAISE FOR DONALD E. WESTLAKE AND THE DORTMUNDER NOVELS

"Is any mystery writer more adept at turning murder into mirth or conjuring up more hilarious hokum than Westlake in his Dortmunder series? I doubt it."

—*Chicago Sunday Sun-Times*

"Westlake is a versatile thriller master."

—*Entertainment Weekly*

"I'm always glad to see John Dortmunder again. . . . It's a kinder, gentler underworld we visit when we ride with Donald Westlake."

—*Charlotte Observer*

"Westlake is equally at home with comedy ranging from slapstick to satire, and with melodrama that runs the gamut from chiller to thriller."

—*San Diego Union-Tribune*

"Westlake has a special genius."

—*Booklist*

THIEVES'
DOZEN

By Donald E. Westlake

NOVELS

Money for Nothing • Put a Lid on It • The Hook • The Ax
Humans • Sacred Monster • A Likely Story • Kahawa
Brothers Keepers • I Gave at the Office • Adios, Scheherazade
Up Your Banners

THE DORTMUNDER SERIES

Bad News • What's the Worst That Could Happen? • Don't Ask
Drowned Hopes • Good Behavior • Why Me • Nobody's Perfect
Jimmy the Kid • Bank Shot • The Hot Rock

COMIC CRIME NOVELS

Smoke • Baby, Would I Lie? • Trust Me on This • High Adventure
Castle in the Air • Enough • Dancing Aztecs • Two Much
Help I Am Being Held Prisoner • Cops and Robbers
Somebody Owes Me Money • Who Stole Sassi Manoon?
God Save the Mark • The Spy in the Ointment • The Busy Body
The Fugitive Pigeon

CRIME NOVELS

Pity Him Afterwards • Killy • 361 • Killing Time • The Mercenaries

JUVENILE

Philip

WESTERN

Gangway (with Brian Garfield)

REPORTAGE

Under an English Heaven

SHORT STORIES

Tomorrow's Crimes • Levine
The Curious Facts Preceding My Execution and Other Fictions
A Good Story and Other Stories

ANTHOLOGY

Once Against the Law (coedited with William Tenn)

DONALD E. WESTLAKE

THIEVES' DOZEN

NEW YORK   BOSTON

This book is a work of fiction. Names, characters, places, and incidents are the product of the author's imagination or are used fictitiously. Any resemblance to actual events, locales, or persons, living or dead, is coincidental.

"Ask a Silly Question," first published in *Playboy*, February 1981, copyright Donald E. Westlake.

"Horse Laugh," first published in *Playboy*, June 1986, copyright Donald E. Westlake.

"Too Many Crooks," first published in *Playboy*, August 1989, copyright Donald E. Westlake.

"A Midsummer Daydream," first published in *Playboy*, May 1990, copyright Donald E. Westlake.

"The Dortmunder Workout," first published in the *New York Times Magazine*, April 29, 1990, copyright Donald E. Westlake.

Copyright information continued on page 184.

Mysterious Press
Warner Books

Time Warner Book Group
1271 Avenue of the Americas, New York, NY 10020
Visit our Web site at www.twbookmark.com.

The Mysterious Press name and logo are registered trademarks of Warner Books.

Printed in the United States of America

Library of Congress Cataloging-in-Publication Data

Westlake, Donald E.
    Thieves' dozen / Donald E. Westlake.
        p.   cm.
        Contents: Ask a silly question—Horse laugh—Too many crooks—A midsummer's daydream—The Dortmunder workout—Party animal—Give till it hurts—Jumble sale—Now what—Art and craft—Fugue for felons.
        ISBN 0-446-69302-2
        1. Dortmunder (Fictitious character)—Fiction.   2. Detective and mystery stories, American.   I. Title.

    PS3573.E9T47   2004
    813'.54—dc22

                                                    2003070612

Book design and text composition by SD Designs
Cover design by Tony Greco

CONTENTS

DORTMUNDER AND ME,
IN SHORT

WHEN JOHN DORTMUNDER AND I FIRST TEAMED UP, IN 1967, neither of us had any idea what we were letting ourselves in for. In fact, at first, it didn't look as though the partnership would get off the ground.

It all began when my regular guy stood me up. I have been, intermittently, a writer known as Richard Stark, who chronicles the incidents in the life of a character called only Parker. In 1967, Parker refused the role I'd planned for him in what was supposed to have been his next book; he thought it was beneath his dignity. So that's when I first turned, just as a substitute, a temp, a one-time hire, to John Archibald Dortmunder. And all I asked him to do was steal the same emerald six times—piece of cake.

John was willing at first, but after three heists he turned surly and wouldn't play any more, so I put that failed project away and turned to something else, thinking Dortmunder and I were merely a blind date that hadn't panned out. Then, two years later, I came across the partial manuscript in a closet, found Dortmunder in a more accommodating frame of mind now that he'd spent two years in the dark, and together we finished the book. It was called *The Hot Rock*, and it was published in 1970.

After *The Hot Rock* and its ensuing movie, in which I was astonished to learn that Dortmunder was Robert Redford, I thought we were quit of each other. I'm sure neither of us ever expected to cross paths again, or to collaborate on what has become as of this writing a total of eleven novels, and we *certainly* never expected to find ourselves mixed up with short stories.

I'm not quite sure how that latter development came about. Ten years had gone by since I'd finished that first Dortmunder novel, with three more added along the way, when into my head came fragments of an elusive conversation between "an elegant man" and John. It didn't seem to be part of a novel, but then, what was it?

Ask a silly question. No, I mean "Ask a Silly Question," the first John Dortmunder short story, containing the elegant man and his class-ridden attitudes, which *Playboy* published in February 1981. Unlike in the novels, Dortmunder worked single-o in the short story, except for a phone-in from his friend Andy Kelp.

Anyway, it looked to me like a one-off. I wasn't writing short stories that decade, or at least hardly ever, and Dortmunder was clearly more comfortable in a setting where he could have his gang around him. So that was it.

Except. Except it kept happening, one way and another. For instance, I was thinking one day about things John might purloin, and I thought of a horse, and I got a picture in my mind of John Dortmunder and a horse gazing deep into each other's eyes, and I loved it. But I couldn't do it. I haven't met enough horses to be able to write an entire novel about a horse. But, come to think of it, I could write a short story. And did.

More time went by, and then, as occasionally happens (my one link to Joan of Arc), another fragment of conversation wafted through my brain one day in 1988—"What's that noise?" "Maybe it's the wind." "What wind? We're in a tunnel."—and that became "Too Many Crooks," mainly because I wanted to know what those two were doing in a tunnel.

A year later, I myself had occasion to wonder what I was doing in Italy, where, in fact, I was on vacation. The trouble is, I don't know *how* to go on vacation. From what? I don't have a job, I don't have a boss, and if I have a schedule, it's self-imposed and mostly ignored. So there we were, my wife Abby and I, in a rented house in Tuscany for the month of August, and I didn't quite know what to do with myself.

When at a loss, write. The only writing materials around were pen and paper—pen and postcard to begin with, but we up-graded—and so I wound up doing, in longhand, "A Midsummer Daydream," in which John Dortmunder finds himself at loose ends outside New York City, not knowing what to do in this strange locale. I typed it when I got home, since my handwriting looks like a ball of string a kitten has played with, and *Playboy* took that one, too, like the others.

Then there came an anomaly. The Sunday edition of the *New York Times* doesn't weigh enough all by itself to satisfy its editors, so they add special sections now and again, and sometimes this special section is a Health supplement to the *Magazine*. An editor from there phoned me, one day in 1989, wondering if John Dortmunder had any thoughts about health, and I had to admit I didn't know but I'd ask. I did, and when "The Dortmunder Workout" was published, in the Health supplement to the *New York Times Magazine*, in the spring of 1990, John was the only guy in the issue without a sweatband around his brow. The editor told me afterward that the staffers who already knew Dortmunder thought it was a nice piece, but those who hadn't previously met my boy were baffled. Well, that seems fair.

After "The Dortmunder Workout" and its preceding four short stories during the '80s, I expected the two of us would *really* be content from now on to stay forever in the land of long-form, but no. A thought came to me, in the early '90s, that a person being chased, wanting to hide, coming across a party, might hide in that milieu not by pretending to be a partygoer—won't the other partygoers realize they don't know him?—but by becoming a member of the caterer's crew, moving among the revelers with little trays of finger food. The other waiters, being temps themselves, won't be surprised to see an unfamiliar face within their group, so maybe the pursued person could blend into this party tapestry until the baying of hounds has receded into the distance. For John and me, it seemed worth the try.

"Party Animal," for thus it came to be called, did not begin life as a Christmas story, but merely as a party story. However, *Playboy* had a hole in its holiday issue that year, and what better thing do these people have to celebrate than Christmas? So there we have it.

But then, just to complicate things, the next story John and I embarked on was supposed from the very beginning to be about Christmas. I, who can go years without writing a word about Christmas, and John Dortmunder, who dislikes all holidays indiscriminately because everybody's home, combined to make two Christmas stories in a row.

What happened, I got a call from Otto Penzler, founder of Mysterious Press and owner-operator of the Mysterious Bookshop in Manhattan. He explained that his store had a large mail-order business, that the Christmas season was a potent part of that business, and that he'd thought it would be a nice thing to give his regular customers a bonus, a Christmas present of a short story just for them, once every year, each time out with a different writer they might have heard of. Would I like to write the first one?

I consulted with John, and it turned out he'd always wanted to attend the occasional poker game in which Otto and I and a few others are regulars (it's the game itself, sans scheduled time slot or location, that's irregular), and which is sometimes played in the library behind Otto's shop. So John dropped in, played the hand he was dealt, and "Give Till It Hurts" was the result.

Until this point, all these briefer travails had involved John either by himself or in company with Andy Kelp, but no one else from his extended unfamily had ever shown up. But there was one particular character who'd appeared in a few of the novels—a fence with a heart of tin, a sourpuss named Arnie Albright—and in thinking about him one day I saw a little something *he* could do that didn't lend itself to novel treatment, but which could certainly be the basis for a short story.

It was, but it wasn't right for *Playboy*. I thought, however, it might be right for *The Armchair Detective*, a very good magazine devoted to the mystery genre, and to my delight they thought so, too, so that's where "Jumble Sale" was published.

That story, set in Arnie Albright's charming apartment, was written in the fall of 1993, twelve years after John and I had first entered the lists of the ten-yard dash. In that time, we'd combined for seven short stories and one workout, and until then I'd had no particular goal in mind beyond each event, assuming every time that this story was the last, that John and I had longer fish to fry. But now it occurred to me that if we combined on just two or three additional mini-sagas, we'd have enough for a collection. So all I had to do was think of two or three more stories.

I don't know how it is with anybody else, but I can never think about what I'm supposed to think about. Dortmunder short stories had come along and come along, never anticipated and never particularly needed, but as soon as I decided I *should* do another Dortmunder short story, I couldn't think of one. Here I was, most of the way across the stream, with only two flat stones to touch to reach the other bank, and not a flat stone could I find anywhere inside my head (which is usually full of them).

It wasn't until more than four years later, when I'd given up on the idea of a Dortmunder collection or any more Dortmunder short stories for any reason at all, a time when I was supposed to be thinking about something else entirely, when here it came, and it couldn't have been more simple. John would leave home on a little errand, that's all. "Now What?" the story was called, and it was back to Dortmunder working solo, and all he was trying to do was get from point A to point B. Well, he got back to *Playboy*; he could settle for that.

And we found the same home with the final story in this assemblage, "Art and Craft," in which, I admit, John did poach on territory not normally his own. Maybe it's that he's been associated in bookstores and libraries with detective stories and their sleuths all these years—though, in his case, mostly in rebuttal—that led him at last to make, in "Art and Craft," the kind of observation of tiny detail that's usually the province of cerebral plainclothesmen and grandmas with cats. Still, his use of the technique remains peculiarly his own.

And I guess Dortmunder remains peculiarly mine, at whatever length. Originally, he was just passing through. He wasn't expected to have legs, and yet here he is, still domitable but bowed, apprentice, it would appear, of both the extended romp and the quick hit, the perhaps-not-exactly-surgical strike.

Through these years of John Dortmunder's brief encounters, there has remained one constant, and her name is Alice Turner. She was the fiction editor at *Playboy*, where seven of the stories herein first appeared, and through all these travails she continued to look upon John and me with bemused disbelief followed by stoical acceptance. (Acceptance is an important quality in a magazine editor.) Her suggestions have been not onerous and always to the point, and have definitely improved the product. She's also a terrific person who, in her off-hours, wrote a history of Hell, so what's not to like?

Speaking of which, some years ago, as a result of a contractual contretemps with a motion picture studio (the closest thing to evil incarnate left in this secular age), it looked for a while as though I might either have to stop writing about John entirely—a horrible thought—or change his name, which the harpies were claiming for themselves. A pseudonym for John seemed a possibility, since he'd been known to sail under colors other than his own once or twice already, but when I went to *choose* that new name, nothing worked. John Dortmunder was John Dortmunder, damn it, and nobody else.

After brooding for a month, I finally settled on the name Rumsey, which I had found on an exit sign on the Saw Mill River Parkway, north of New York City. Rumsey seemed to me closest in feeling, in philosophy, in weltanschauung (not to mention weltschmerz) to Dortmunder.

I typed out the name a few times: John Rumsey. John Rumsey. John Rumsey. Hmmm.

Fortunately, the evil empire's shadow receded from my peaceful village, so Dortmunder could go on being Dortmunder after all, and once that happened, I could admit to myself that even Rumsey wasn't a completely satisfying substitute. The problem is, John Rumsey is short. John Dortmunder is of average height, but John Rumsey is short. If the guys were to get together in the back room of the O.J. Bar & Grill to scope and scheme some new outrage, John Rumsey would be the shortest guy in the joint. Don't ask me how I know; I know.

Hey. Maybe this is really Rumsey, here in this collection. You think?

THIEVES'
DOZEN

Ask a Silly Question

Art theft, of course," said the elegant man, "has been overdone. By now it's thoroughly boring."

Dortmunder didn't say anything. His business was theft, of art or whatever else had value, and he'd never supposed it was meant to be exciting. Nor, while tiptoeing around darkened halls in guarded buildings with his pockets full of stolen goods, had he ever found boredom much of a problem.

The elegant man sighed. "What do people of your sort drink?" he asked.

"Bourbon," Dortmunder said. "Water. Coca-Cola. Orange juice. Beer."

"Bourbon," the elegant man told one of the two plug-uglies who'd brought Dortmunder here. "And sherry for me."

"Coffee," Dortmunder went on. "Sometimes Gallo Burgundy. Vodka. Seven-Up. Milk."

"How do you prefer your bourbon?" the elegant man asked.

"With ice and water. People of my sort also drink Hi-C, Scotch, lemonade, Nyquil—"

"Do you drink Perrier?"

"No," said Dortmunder.

"Ah," said the elegant man, closing the subject with his preconceptions intact. "Now," he said, "I suppose you're wondering why we all gathered you here."

"I got an appointment uptown," Dortmunder answered. He was feeling mulish. When a simple walk to the subway turns into an incident with two plug-uglies, a gun in the back, a shoving into a limousine outfitted with liveried chauffeur beyond the closed glass partition, a run up the stocking of Manhattan to the East Sixties, a swallowing up into a town house *with* a garage *with* an electronically operated door, and an interview at gunpoint with a tall, slender, painfully well-dressed, 60ish, white-haired, white-mustached elegant man in a beautifully appointed and very masculine den imported intact from Bloomingdale's, a person has a right to feel mulish. "I'm already late for my appointment," Dortmunder pointed out.

"I'll try to be brief," the elegant man promised. "My father— who, by the way, was once Secretary of the Treasury of this great land, under Teddy Roosevelt—always impressed upon me the wisdom of obtaining expert advice before undertaking any project, of whatever size or scope. I have always followed that injunction."

"Uh-huh," said Dortmunder.

"The exigencies of life having made it necessary for me," the elegant man continued, "to engage for once in the practice of grand larceny, in the form of burglary, I immediately sought out a professional in the field to advise me. You."

"I reformed," Dortmunder said. "I made some mistakes in my youth, but I paid my debt to society and now I'm reformed."

"Of course," said the elegant man. "Ah, here are our drinks. Come along, I have something to show you."

It was a dark and lumpy statue, about four feet tall, of a moody teenaged girl dressed in curtains and sitting on a tree trunk. "Beautiful, isn't it?" the elegant man said, gazing fondly at the thing.

Beauty was outside Dortmunder's visual spectrum. "Yeah," he said, and looked around this subterranean room, which had been fitted out like a cross between a den and a museum. Bookcases alternated with paintings on the walls, and antique furniture shared the polished wood floor with statuary, some on pedestals, some, like this bronze of a young girl, on low platforms. Dortmunder and the elegant man and the armed plug-uglies had come down here by elevator: apparently, the only route in and out. There were no windows and the air had the flat blanketlike quality of tight temperature and humidity control.

"It's a Rodin," the elegant man was saying. "One of my wiser acquisitions, in my youth." His mouth forming a practiced *moue*, he said, "One of my *less* wise acquisitions, more recently, was a flesh-and-blood young woman who did me the disservice of becoming my wife."

"I really got an appointment uptown," Dortmunder said.

"More recently still," the elegant man persisted, "we came to a particularly bitter and unpleasant parting of the ways, Moira and I. As a part of the resulting settlement, the little bitch got this nymph here. But she *didn't* get it."

"Uh-huh," Dortmunder said.

"I have friends in the art world," the elegant man went on, "and all men have sympathizers where grasping ex-wives are concerned. Several years earlier, I'd had a mold made of this piece, and from it an exact copy had been cast in the same grade of bronze. A virtually identical copy; not quite museum quality, of course, but aesthetically just as pleasing as the original."

"Sure," said Dortmunder.

"It was that copy I gave to Moira; having, of course, first bribed the expert she'd brought in to appraise the objects she was looting from me. The other pieces I gave her with scarcely a murmur, but my nymph? Never!"

"Ah," said Dortmunder.

"All was well," the elegant man said. "I kept my nymph, the one and only true original from Rodin's plaster form, with the touch of the sculptor's hand full upon it. Moira had the copy, pleased with the thought of its being the original, cheered by the memory of having done me in the eye. A happy ending for everyone, you might have said."

"Uh-huh," said Dortmunder.

"But not an ending at all, unfortunately." The elegant man shook his head. "It has come to my attention, *very* belatedly, that tax problems have forced Moira to make a gift of the Rodin nymph to the Museum of Modern Art. Perhaps I ought to explain that even I cannot with any certainty bribe an appraiser from the Museum of Modern Art."

"He'll tell," Dortmunder said.

"He will, in the argot of the underworld," the elegant man said, "spill the beans."

"That isn't the argot of the underworld," Dortmunder told him.

"No matter. The point is, my one recourse, it seems to me, is to enter Moira's town house and make off with the copy."

"Makes sense," Dortmunder agreed.

The elegant man pointed at his nymph. "Pick that up," he said.

Dortmunder frowned, looking for the butcher's thumb.

"Go ahead," the elegant man insisted. "It won't bite."

Dortmunder handed his bourbon and water to one of the plug-uglies; then hesitant, unfamiliar with the process of lifting teenaged girls dressed in curtains—whether of bronze or anything else—he grasped this one by the chin and one elbow and lifted . . . and it didn't move. "Uh," said Dortmunder, visions of hernias blooming in his head.

"You see the problem," the elegant man said, while the muscles in Dortmunder's arms and shoulders and back and groin all quivered from the unexpected shock. "My nymph weighs five hundred twenty-six pounds. As does Moira's copy, give or take a few ounces."

"Heavy," agreed Dortmunder. He took back his drink and drank.

"The museum's expert arrives tomorrow afternoon," the elegant man said touching his white mustache. "If I am to avoid discomfort—possibly even public disgrace—I must remove Moira's copy from her possession tonight."

Dortmunder said, "And you want me to do it?"

"No, no, not at all." The elegant man waved his elegant fingers. "My associates"—meaning the plug-uglies—"and I will, as you would say, pull the scam."

"That's not what I'd say," Dortmunder told him.

"No matter, no matter. What we wish from you, Mr. Dortmunder, is simply your expertise. Your professional opinion. Come along." The elevator door opened to his elegant touch. "Care for another bourbon? Of course you do."

"Fortunately," the elegant man said, "I kept the architect's plans and models even though I lost the town house itself to Moira."

Dortmunder and his host and one plug-ugly (the other was off getting more bourbon and sherry) stood now in a softly glowing dining room overlooking a formal brick-and-greenery rear garden. On the antique refectory table dominating the room stood two model houses next to a roll of blueprints. The tiniest model, barely six inches tall and built solid of balsa wood with windows and other details painted on, was placed on an aerial photograph to the same scale, apparently illustrating the block in which the finished house would stand. The larger, like a child's dollhouse, was over two feet tall, with what looked like real glass in its windows and even some furniture in the rooms within. Both models were of a large, nearly square house with a high front stoop, four stories tall, with a big square many-paned skylight in the center of the roof.

Dortmunder looked at the big model, then at the small, then at the photograph of the street. "This is in New York?"

"Just a few blocks from here."

"Huh," said Dortmunder, thinking of his own apartment.

"You see the skylight," suggested the elegant man.

"Yeah."

"It can be opened in good weather. There's an atrium on the second level. You know what an atrium is?"

"No."

"It's a kind of garden, within the house. Here, let me show you."

The larger model was built in pieces, which could be disassembled. The roof came off first, showing bedrooms and baths all around a big square opening coinciding with the skylight. The top floor came off, was set aside and showed a third floor given over to a master bedroom suite and a bookcase-lined den, around the continuing square atrium hole. The details impressed even Dortmunder. "This thing must have cost as much as the real house," he said.

The elegant man smiled. "Not quite," he said, lifting off the third floor. And here was the bottom of the atrium—fancy word for air shaft, Dortmunder decided—a formal garden like the one outside these real-life dining-room windows, with a fountain and stone paths. The living and dining rooms in the model were open to the atrium. "Moira's copy," the elegant man said, pointing at the garden, "is just about there."

"Tricky," Dortmunder commented.

"There are twelve steps down from the atrium level to the sidewalk in front. The rear garden is sunk deeper, below ground level."

"Very tricky."

"Ah, our drinks," the elegant man said, taking his, "and not a moment too soon." He sipped elegantly and said, "Mr. Dortmunder, the workman is worthy of his hire. I shall now outline to you our plans and our reasoning. I ask you to give us your careful attention, to advise us of any flaws in our thinking and to suggest whatever improvements come to your professional mind. In return, I will pay you—in cash, of course—one thousand dollars."

"And drive me uptown," Dortmunder said. "I'm really late for my appointment."

"Agreed."

"OK, then," Dortmunder said, and looked around for a place to sit down.

"Oh, come along," said the elegant man. "We might as well be comfortable."

Tall, narrow windows in the living room overlooked a tree-lined expensive block. Long sofas in ecru crushed velvet faced each other on the Persian carpet, amid glass-topped tables, modern lamps and antique bric-a-brac. In a Millet over the mantel, a French farmer of the last century endlessly pushed his barrowload of hay through a narrow barn door. The elegant man might have lost his atriummed town house to the scheming Moira, but he was still doing OK. No welfare housing necessary.

With a fresh drink to hand, Dortmunder sat on a sofa and listened. "We've made three plans," the elegant man said, as Dortmunder wondered who this "we" was he kept talking about; surely not the plug-uglies, giants with the brains of two-by-fours, sitting around now on chair arms like a rock star's bodyguards. "Our first plan, perhaps still feasible, involves that skylight and a helicopter. I have access to a heli—"

"Loud," Dortmunder said.

The elegant man paused, as though surprised, then smiled. "That's right," he said.

Dortmunder gave him a flat look. "Was that a test? You wanna see if I'll just say, 'Yeah, yeah, that's fine, give me my grand and take me uptown,' is that it?"

"To some extent," agreed the elegant man placidly. "Of course, apart from the noise—a dead giveaway to the entire neighborhood, naturally, the house would swarm with police before we'd so much as attached the grapple—still, apart from that noise problem, a helicopter *is* quite an attractive solution. At night, from above—"

"Illegal," interrupted Dortmunder.

"Eh?"

"You can't fly a helicopter over Manhattan after dark. There's a law. Never break a law you don't intend to break: people get grabbed for a traffic violation, and what they're really doing is robbing a bank. That kind of thing. It happens all the time."

"I see." The elegant man looked thoughtful. Smoothing back his silver locks, he said, "Every trade is more complicated than it appears, isn't it?"

"Yeah," said Dortmunder. "What's plan number two?"

"Ah, yes." The elegant man regained his pleased look. "This involves the front door."

"How many people in this house?"

"None." Then the elegant man made a dismissing finger wave, saying, "The staff, of course. But they're all downstairs. It's soundproofed down there and servants sleep like the dead, anyway."

"If you say so. Where's this Moira?"

"She *should* be in England, mired on the M four," the elegant man said, looking extremely irritated, "but the delay I'd arranged for her to undergo didn't quite take place. As a result, she is probably at this very moment boarding her flight to New York. She'll be here sometime early tomorrow morning." Shrugging away his annoyance, he said, "Nevertheless, we still have all of tonight. Plan number two, as I started to say, has us forcing entry through the front door. Three strong men"—with a graceful hand gesture to include both himself and the silent plug-uglies—"with some difficulty, can jog the statue onto a low wheeled dolly. Out front, we shall have a truck equipped with a winch, whose long cable will reach as far as the atrium. The winch can pull the statue on the dolly through the house and down a metal ramp from the head of the stairs to the interior of the truck."

"That sounds OK," said Dortmunder. "What's the problem?"

"The guard," the elegant man explained, "outside the embassy next door."

"Oh," said Dortmunder. "And if you get rid of the guard. . . ."

"We create an international incident. A side effect even more severe than the breaking of helicopter-at-night laws."

Dortmunder shook his head. "Tell me about plan number three."

"We effect entry through the rear, from the house on the next block. We set various incendiary devices and we burn the place down."

Dortmunder frowned. "Metal doesn't burn," he objected.

"A flaw we'd noticed ourselves," the elegant man admitted.

Dortmunder drank bourbon and gave his host a look of disgust. "You don't have any plan at all," he said.

"We have no *good* plans," the elegant man said. "Would you have a suggestion of your own?"

"For a thousand dollars?" Dortmunder sipped bourbon and looked patiently at the elegant man.

Who smiled, a bit sadly. "I see what you mean," he said. "Say two thousand."

"Say ten thousand," Dortmunder suggested.

"I couldn't possibly say ten thousand. I might find it possible to say twenty-five hundred."

It took three minutes and many little delicate silences before Dortmunder and the elegant man reached the $5000 honorarium both had settled on in advance.

The interior ladder down from the skylight had been so cunningly integrated into the decor of the house that it was practically useless; tiny rungs, irregularly spaced, far too narrow and curving frighteningly down the inside of the domed ceiling. Dortmunder, who had a perfectly rational fear of heights, inched his way downward, prodded by the plug-ugly behind him and encouraged by the plug-ugly ahead, while trying not to look between his shoes at the tiny shrubbery and statuary and ornamental fountain three long stories below.

What a lot of air there is in an atrium!

Attaining the safety of the top-floor floor, Dortmunder turned to the elegant man, who had come first down the ladder with an astonishing spryness and lack of apprehension, and told him, "This isn't fair, that's all. I'm here under protest."

"Of course you are," the elegant man said. "That's why my associates had to show you their revolvers. But surely for five thousand dollars, we can expect you to be present while your rather ingenious scheme is being worked out."

A black satchel, tied about with a hairy thick yellow rope, descended past in small spasms, lowered by the plug-ugly who was remaining on the roof. "I never been so late for an appointment in my life," Dortmunder said. "I should of been uptown hours ago."

"Come along," the elegant man said, "we'll find you a phone, you can call and explain. But please invent an explanation; the truth should not be telephoned."

Dortmunder, who had never telephoned the truth and who hardly ever even presented the truth in person, made no reply, but followed the elegant man and the other plug-ugly down the winding staircase to the main floor, where the plug-ugly with muttered curses removed the black satchel from the ornamental fountain. "You shouldn't get that stuff wet," Dortmunder pointed out.

"Accidents will happen," the elegant man said carelessly, while the plug-ugly continued to mutter. "Let's find you a telephone."

They found it in the living room, near the tall front windows, on a charming antique desk inlaid with green leather. Seated at this, Dortmunder could look diagonally out the window and see the guard strolling in front of the embassy next door. An empty cab drifted by, between the lines of parked cars. The elegant man went back to the atrium and Dortmunder picked up the phone and dialed.

"O.J. Bar and Grill, Rollo speaking."

"This is Dortmunder."

"Who?"

"The bourbon and water."

"Oh, yeah. Say, your pals are in the back. They're waiting for you, huh?"

"Yeah," Dortmunder said. "Let me talk to Ke— The other bourbon and water."

"Sure."

A police car oozed by; the embassy guard waved at it. Opening the desk drawer, Dortmunder found a gold bracelet set with emeralds and rubies; he put it in his pocket. Behind him, a sudden loud mechanical rasping sound began; he put his thumb in his other ear.

"Hello? Dortmunder?" Kelp's voice.

"Yeah," Dortmunder said.

"You're late."

"I got tied up. With some people."

"Something going on?"

"I'll tell you later."

"You sound like you're in a body shop."

"A what?"

"Where they fix cars. You don't have a car, do you?"

"No," Dortmunder said. The rasping sound was *very* loud.

"That's very sensible," Kelp said. "What with the energy crisis, and inflation, and being in a city with first-rate mass transportation, it doesn't make any sense to own your own car."

"Sure," Dortmunder said. "What I'm calling about—"

"Any time you need a car," Kelp said, "you can just go pick one up."

"That's right," Dortmunder said. "About tonight—"

"So what are you doing in a body shop?"

The rasping sound, or something, was getting on Dortmunder's nerves. "I'll tell you later," he said.

"You'll be along soon?"

"No, I might be stuck here a couple hours. Maybe we should make the meet tomorrow night."

"No problem," Kelp said. "And if you break loose, we can still do it tonight."

"You guys don't have to hang around," Dortmunder told him.

"That's OK. We're having a nice discussion on religion and politics. See you later."

"Right," said Dortmunder.

In the atrium, they were cutting the nymph's head off. As Dortmunder came back from his phone call, the girl's head nodded once, then fell with a splash into the fountain. As the plug-ugly switched off the saw, the elegant man turned toward Dortmunder a face of anguish, saying, "It's like seeing a human being cut up before your eyes. Worse. Were she flesh and blood, I could at least imagine she was Moira."

"That thing's loud," Dortmunder said.

"Not outside," the elegant man assured him. "Because of traffic noise, the façade was soundproofed. Also the floor; the servants won't hear a thing."

The plug-ugly having wrapped the decapitated head in rope, he switched on his saw again and attacked the nymph, this time at her waistline. The head, meantime, peering raffishly through circlets of yellow rope, rose slowly roofward, hauled from above.

Dortmunder, having pointed out to the elegant man that *removal* of this statue was all that mattered, that its postoperative condition was unimportant, had for his $5000 suggested they cut it into totable chunks and remove it via the roof. Since, like most cast-bronze statues, it was hollow rather than solid, the dismembering was certainly within the range of the possible.

Dortmunder had first thought in terms of an industrial laser, which would make a fast, clean and absolutely silent cut, but the elegant man's elegant contacts did not include access to a laser, so Dortmunder had fallen back on the notion of an acetylene torch. (Everybody in Dortmunder's circle had an acetylene torch.) But there, too, the elegant man had turned out to be deficient, and it was only after exhaustive search of the garage that this large saber saw and several metal-cutting blades had been found. Well, it was better than a pocket-knife, though not so quiet.

The head fell from the sky into the fountain, splashing everybody with water.

The plug-ugly with the saw turned it off, lifted his head and spoke disparagingly to his partner on the roof, who replied in kind. The elegant man raised his own voice, in French, and when the plug-uglies ceased maligning each other, he said, "*I* shall bind the parts."

The nearer plug-ugly gave him a sullen look. "That's brain-work, *I* guess," he said, switched on the saber saw and stabbed the nymph in the belly with it. Renewed racket buried the elegant man's response.

It was too loud here. From Dortmunder's memory of the model of this house, the kitchen should be through the dining room and turn right. While the elegant man fumbled with the bronze head, Dortmunder strolled away. Passing through the dining room, he pocketed an antique oval ivory cameo frame.

Dortmunder paused in the preparation of his second *pâté* and swiss on rye with Dijon mustard—this kitchen contained neither peanut butter *nor* jelly—when the racket of saber saw was abruptly replaced by the racket of angry voices. Among them was a voice undoubtedly female. Dortmunder sighed, closed the sandwich, carried it in his left hand and went through to the atrium, where a woman surrounded by Louis Vuitton suitcases was yelling at the top of her voice at the elegant man, who was yelling just as loudly right back. The plug-ugly stood to one side, openmouthed but silent, the saber saw also silent in his hand, hovering over the statue stub, now reduced to tree trunk, knees, shins, feet, toes, base and a bit of curtain hem.

This was clearly the ex-wife, home ahead of schedule. The elegant man seemed unable to do *anything* right. In the semi-darkness of the dining-room doorway, Dortmunder ate his sandwich and listened and watched.

The screaming was merely that at first, screaming, with barely any rational words identifiable in the mix, but the ex-wife's first impulse to make lots of noise was soon overtaken by the full realization that her statue was *all cut to pieces;* gradually, her shrieks faded away to gasps and then to mere panting, until at last she merely stood in stunned silence, staring at the destruction, while the elegant man also ceased to bray. Regaining his composure and his elegance, he readjusted his cuffs and, with barely a tremor in his voice, he said, "Moira, I admit you have me at a disadvantage."

"You—you—" But she wasn't capable of description, not yet, not with the butchery right here in front of her.

"An explanation is in order," the elegant man acknowledged, "but first let me reassure you on one point: That Rodin has not been destroyed. You will still, I'm afraid, be able to turn it over to the populace."

"You bluh—you—"

"My presence here," the elegant man continued, as though his ex-wife's paralysis were an invitation to go on, "is the result of an earlier deception, at the time of our separation. I'm afraid I must admit to you now that I bribed Grindle at that time to accept on your behalf not the original but a copy of the Rodin—this copy, in fact."

The ex-wife took a deep breath. She looked away from the bronze carnage and gazed at the elegant man. "You bloody fool," she said, having at last recaptured her voice, and speaking now almost in a conversational tone. "You bloody self-satisfied fool, do you think you *invented* bribery?"

A slight frown wrinkled the elegant man's features. "I beg your pardon?"

"Beg Rodin's," she told him. "*You* could only bribe Grindle with cash. When he told me your proposition, I saw no reason why he shouldn't take it."

"You—you—" Now it was the elegant man who was losing the power of speech.

"And, having taken your bribe *and* mine," she went inexorably on, "he pronounced the false true before reversing the statues. *That*," pointing at the shins and tree trunk, "was the original."

"Impossible!" The elegant man had begun to blink. His tie was askew. "Grindle wouldn't—I've kept the—"

"*You bloody* FOOL!" And the woman reached for a handy piece of luggage—toilet case, swamp-colored, speckled with someone else's initials, retail $364.50—and hurled it at her ex-husband, who ducked, bellowed and reached for the late nymph's bronze thigh with which to riposte. The woman sidestepped and the thigh rolled across the atrium, coming to a stop at Dortmunder's feet. He looked down at it, saw the glint of something shiny on the rough inside surface and hunkered down for a closer look. At the foundry, when they'd covered the removable plaster interior with wax prior to pouring the bronze, maybe some French coin, now old and valuable, had got stuck in the wax and then transferred to the bronze. Dortmunder peered in at the thing, reaching out one hand to turn the thigh slightly to improve the light, then running his finger tips over the shiny thing, testing to see if it would come loose. But it was well and firmly fixed in place.

The rasp of the saber saw once more snarled; Dortmunder, looking up, saw that the woman had it now, and was chasing her ex-husband around the plants and flowers with it, while the plug-ugly stood frozen, pretending to be a floor lamp. Dortmunder stood, mouthed the last of his sandwich, retraced his steps to the kitchen and went out the window.

The far-off sound of sirens was just audible when he reached the pay phone at the corner and called again the O.J. Bar & Grill. When Kelp came on the phone, Dortmunder said, "The guys still there?"

"Sure. You on your way?"

"No. I got a new thing over here on the East Side. You and the guys meet me at Park and Sixty-fifth."

"Sure. What's up?"

"Just a little breaking and entering."

"The place is empty?"

Down the block, police cars were massing in front of Moira's house. "Oh, yeah," Dortmunder said, "it's empty. I don't think the owner's gonna be back for years."

"Something valuable?"

There weren't two copies of the Rodin, no; there was one original, one copy. And the elegant man had been right about ex-husbands' getting the sympathy vote. The hired expert had accepted bribes from both parties, but he'd made his own decision when it came to distributing the real and the fake Rodins. In Dortmunder's mind's eye, he saw again the shiny thing hidden within the nymph's thigh. It was the flip-off ring from a thoroughly modern beer can. "It's valuable OK," he said. "But it's kind of heavy. On the way over, steal a truck."

HORSE LAUGH

DORTMUNDER LOOKED AT THE HORSE. THE HORSE LOOKED AT Dortmunder. "Ugly goddamn thing," Dortmunder commented, while the horse just rolled his eyes in disbelief.

"Not that one," the old coot said. "We're looking for a black stallion."

"In the dark," Dortmunder pointed out. "Anyway, all horses look the same to me."

"It's not how they look," the old coot said, "it's how they run. And Dire Straits could run the ass off a plug like this one. Which is why he won't be out here in the night air with these glue factories. We'll find Dire Straits in one of them barns down there."

That was another thing rubbing Dortmunder the wrong way—the names that horses get saddled with. Abby's Elbow, Nuff Said, Dreadful Summit, Dire Straits. If you were going out to the track, where the horses were almost irrelevant to the occasion, where the point was to drink beer and bet money and socialize a little and make small jokes like, "I hope I break even today; I could use the cash," it didn't matter much that you were betting 30 across the board on something called Giant Can and that you had to wait for a bunch of horses outdoors somewhere to run around in a big oval before you found out if you had won. But here, in the darkest wilds of New Jersey, on a ranch barely 60 miles from New York City, surrounded by all these huge, nervous creatures, pawing and snorting and rolling their eyes, out here breathing this moist, smelly air, walking in mud or worse, it just capped Dortmunder's discontent that these dangerous furry barrels on sticks were named Picasso's Revenge and How'm I Doin'?

From some distance away, Andy Kelp's cautious voice rose into the rich air, saying, "There's more down that way. I heard some go, 'Snushfurryblurryblurryblurry.'"

"That's a whicker," the old coot said, as though anybody gave a damn.

"I don't care if it's mohair," Kelp told him. "Let's do this and get out of here. I'm a city boy myself."

The edge of nervousness and impatience in Kelp's voice was music to Dortmunder's ears. It was Kelp who'd brought him into this caper in the first place, so if Dortmunder was going to suffer, it was nice to know that his best friend was also unhappy and discontented.

It was the eternally optimistic Kelp who had first met the old coot, named Hiram Rangle, and brought him around to the O.J. Bar & Grill on Amsterdam Avenue one night to meet Dortmunder and discuss a matter of possible mutual benefit. "I work for this fella," Hiram Rangle had said in his raspy old-coot voice, his faded-blue eyes staring suspiciously out of his leathery brown face. "But I'm not gonna tell you his name."

"You don't have to tell me anything," Dortmunder said. He was a little annoyed in a general way, having had a series of things go wrong lately—not important, doesn't matter—and it hadn't been *his* idea to take this meeting. Over at the bar, the regulars were discussing the latest advances in psychotherapy— "It's called A version, and it's a way to make you have a different version of how you see women"; "I like the version I got"—and Dortmunder was sitting here with this old coot, a skinny little guy in deerskin jacket and flannel shirt and corduroy pants and yellow boots big enough to garage a Honda, and the coot was telling him what he *would* tell him and what he *wouldn't* tell him. "You and my pal Andy here," Dortmunder said, lifting his glass of bar bourbon, "can go talk to the crowd at the bar for all I care."

"Aw, come on, John," Kelp said. He totally wanted this thing to happen, and he leaned his sharp-featured face over the scarred corner table, as though to draw Dortmunder and the old coot together by sheer force of personality. He said, "This is a good deal for everybody. Let Hiram tell you about it."

"He says he doesn't want to."

"I got to be careful, that's all," the old coot said, sipping defensively at his Tsing-Tao.

"Then don't come to joints like this," Dortmunder advised him.

"*Tell* the man, Hiram," Kelp said. "That's what you're here for."

Hiram took a breath and put down his glass. "What it comes down to is," he said, "we want to steal a horse."

They wanted to steal a horse. What it came down to was, the old coot worked for some guy who was full of schemes and scams, and one of them was a long-range plot involving this race horse, Dire Straits, on whom Dortmunder could remember having dropped some rent money some years back on a couple of those rare occasions when Dire Straits had finished out of the running. It seemed that Dire Straits, having in his racing career won many millions for many people (and having lost a few kopecks for Dortmunder), had now been put out to stud, which, as described by the old coot, sounded like a retirement plan better than most. These days, Dire Straits hung around with some other male horses on a nice green-grass farm over near Short Hills, New Jersey—"If they're short, why do they call them hills?" Dortmunder had wanted to know, which was something else the old coot didn't have an answer for—and from time to time, the owners of female horses paid the owners of Dire Straits great big sackfuls of money for him to go off and party. It seems there was a theory that the sons and daughters of fast horses would also be fast, and a lot of money changed hands on that theory.

Well, the schemer, Hiram Rangle's anonymous boss, owned some fairly fast horses himself, but nothing in the Dire Straits class, so his idea was to kidnap Dire Straits and put him to work partying with his own female horses; and then, when the female horses had sons and daughters, the schemer would put down on the birth certificate some slow-moving plater as the father. Then, when the sons and daughters grew up enough to start to run, which would take only a couple of years, the odds against them would be very long, because of their alleged parentage; but because Dire Straits was their real daddy, they would run like crazy, and the schemer would bet on them and make a bundle. In a few months, of course, the odds would adjust to the horses' actual track records; but by then, the schemer would be home free. With three or four of Dire Straits' disguised kiddies hitting the turf every year and maybe another five or six years of active partying left in his life, it was a scheme that, as a fellow might say, had legs.

Kelp put it slightly differently: "It's like *The Prince and the Pauper,* where you don't know it, but your real daddy's the king."

"I think we're talking about horses here," Dortmunder told him.

Kelp shook his head. "You never see the romantic side," he said.

"I'll leave that to Dire Straits," Dortmunder said.

Anyway, it turned out that the one fly in the ointment in the schemer's scheme was the fact that, even with all his hustling and finagling, he'd never in his career done any actual, straightforward, out-and-out theft. He had his scheme, he had his own ranch with his own female horses on it, he had a nice cash cushion to use in making his bets three years down the line, but the one thing he didn't have, and didn't know how to get, was Dire Straits. So one way or another, his hireling, Rangle, had got in touch with Andy Kelp, who had said his friend John Dortmunder was exactly the man to plan and execute a robbery of this delicate and unusual a nature, and that was why this meeting was taking place in the O.J., where over at the bar the regulars were now arguing about whether penis envy was confined to men or if women could have it, too: "How can they? What's the basis of the comparison?"

"I can tell you this much," Hiram Rangle said. "My boss'll pay twenty thousand dollars for Dire Straits. Not to me; I've already got my salary. To the people who help me."

"Ten thousand apiece, John," Kelp pointed out.

"I know how to divide by two, Andy." Dortmunder also knew how to divide by zero, which was how he'd profited from his other operations recently—just a little run of hard luck, nothing worth talking about—which was why he'd finally nodded and said, "I'll look at this horse of yours," and why he was now here in the sultry New Jersey night, ankle-deep in some sort of warm, dark pulpiness, listening to Andy Kelp imitate horse whickers and deciding it was time they found the right animal and got the hell out of there.

Because the problem was that Dire Straits was, in a manner of speaking, in prison. A prison *farm,* actually, with fields and open sky, but a prison nevertheless, with tall fences and locked gates and a fairly complicated route in and out. And breaking into a prison for horses was not much easier than breaking into a prison for people, particularly when the horses involved were also valuable.

V-A-L-U-A-B-L-E. When Kelp first showed Dortmunder the item from the *Daily News* sports pages about how Dire Straits was insured for more than $1,000,000, Dortmunder had said, "A million dollars? Then what do we need with ten grand? Why don't we deal with the insurance company?"

"John, I thought of that," Kelp had said, "but the question is,

Where would we keep it while we negotiated? I've only got the studio apartment, you know."

"Well, May wouldn't let me keep it at our place, I know that much." Dortmunder sighed and nodded. "OK. We'll settle for the ten."

That was last week. This week, on Tuesday, Kelp and Dortmunder and the old coot had driven out through the Holland Tunnel and across New Jersey into the Short Hills area in a Ford Fairlane the old coot had rented, and when they got to the place, this is what they saw. On a wandering country road through rolling countryside covered with the lush greenery of August was a modest Colonial-style sign reading YERBA BUENA RANCH, mounted on a post next to a blacktop road climbing up a low hill toward a white farmhouse visible some distance in through the trees. Kelp, at the wheel, turned in there just to see what would happen, and what happened was that, about halfway to the house—white-rail fences to both sides of the blacktop, more white-rail fences visible in the fields beyond the house—a nice young fellow in blue jeans and a T-shirt with a picture of a horse on it came walking out and smiled pleasantly as Kelp braked to a stop, and then said, "Help you, folks? This is a private road."

"We're looking for Hopatcong," Kelp said, just because the name HOPATCONG on a highway sign had struck him funny. So then, of course, he had to listen to about 18 minutes of instructions on how to get to Hopatcong before they could back up and leave there and drive on up the public road and take the right turn up a very steep hill to a place from which they could look down and see Yerba Buena Ranch spread out below, like a pool table with fences. The ranch was pretty extensive, with irregularly shaped fields all enclosed by those white wooden rails and connected by narrow roads of dirt or blacktop. Here and there were small clusters of trees, like buttons in upholstery, plus about ten brown or white barns and sheds scattered around out behind the main farmhouse. They saw about 30 horses hanging out and watched a little cream-colored pickup truck drive back and forth, and then Dortmunder said, "Doesn't look easy."

Kelp paused in taking many photos of the place to stare in astonishment. "Doesn't look easy? I never saw anything so easy in my life. No alarm system, no armed guards, not even anybody really suspicious."

"You can't put a horse in your pocket," Dortmunder said. "And how do we get a vehicle down in there without somebody noticing?"

"I'll walk him out," the old coot said. "That's no trouble; I know horses."

"Do you know *this* horse?" Dortmunder gestured at the pretty landscape. "They got a whole lot of horses down there."

"I'll know Dire Straits when I see him, don't you worry," the old coot said.

So now was the time to find out if that was an idle boast or not. Using the photos they'd taken from all around the ranch, plus New Jersey road maps and a topographical map that gave Dortmunder a slight headache, he'd figured out the best route to and from the ranch and also the simplest and cleanest way in, which was to start from a small and seldom-traveled county road and hike through somebody else's orchard to the rear of the ranch, then remove two rails from the perimeter fence there. They would go nowhere near the front entrance or the main building. The old coot would go with them to identify Dire Straits and lead him away. Going out, they'd restore the rails to confuse and delay pursuit. The old coot had rented a station wagon and a horse van with room for two horses—Dortmunder and Kelp couldn't get over the idea that they were working with somebody who rented vehicles rather than steal them—and so here they were, around two A.M. on a cloudy, warm night.

But where was Dire Straits?

Could he be off partying somewhere, for heavy money? The old coot insisted no; his anonymous boss had ways of knowing things like that, and Dire Straits was definitely at home these days, resting up between dates.

"He'll be in one of them buildings over there," the old coot said, gesturing vaguely in the general direction of planet Earth.

"I can still hear some back that way," Kelp said. "Now they're going, 'Floor-flor.'"

"That's a snort," the old coot said. "Those old plugs stay outside in good weather, but Dire Straits they keep in his stall, so he stays healthy. Down this way."

So they went down that way, Dortmunder not liking any bit of it. He preferred to think of himself as a professional and for a professional there is always the one right way to do things, as opposed to any number of amateur or wrong ways, and this job just wasn't laying out in a manner that he could take pride in. Having to case the joint from a nearby hilltop, for instance, was far less satisfactory than walking into a bank, or a jewelry wholesaler, or whatever it might be, and pretending to be a messenger with a package for Mr. Hutcheson. "There's no Mr. Hutcheson here." "You sure? Let me call my dispatcher." And so on. Looking things over every second of the time.

You can't show up at a *ranch* with a package for a *horse*.

Nor can you tap a horse's phone or do electronic surveillance on a horse or make up a plaster imitation horse to leave in its place. You can't drill in to the horse from next door or tunnel in from across the street. You can't do a diversionary explosion outside a ranch or use the fire escape or break through the roof. You can't time a horse's movements.

Well, you can, actually, but not the way Dortmunder meant.

The way Dortmunder meant, this horse heist was looking less

and less like what the newspapers call a "well-planned professional robbery" and more and more like hobos sneaking into back yards to steal lawn mowers. Professionally, it was an embarrassment.

"Careful where you walk," the old coot said.

"Too late," Dortmunder told him.

Dortmunder's ideas of farms came from margarine commercials on television and his ideas of ranches from cigarette ads in magazines. This place didn't match either; no three-story-high red barns, no masses of horses running pell-mell past boulders. What you had was these long, low brown buildings scattered among the railed-in fields, and what it mostly reminded Dortmunder of was World War Two prisoner-of-war-camp movies—not a comforting image.

"He'll be in one of these three barns," the old coot said. "I'm pretty sure."

So they entered a long structure with a wide central cement-floored aisle spotted with dirt and straw. A few low-wattage bare bulbs hung from the rough beams above the aisle, and chest-high wooden partitions lined both sides. These were the stalls, about two thirds occupied.

Walking through this first barn, Dortmunder learned several facts about horses: (1) They smell. (2) They breathe, more than anything he'd ever met in his life before. (3) They don't sleep, not even at night. (4) They don't even sit down. (5) They are very curious about people who happen to go by. And (6) they have extremely long necks. When horses in stalls on both sides of Dortmunder stretched out their heads toward him at the same time, wrinkling their black lips to show their big, square tombstone teeth, snuffling and whuffling with those shotgun-barrel noses, sighting at him down those long faces, he realized that the aisle wasn't that wide after all.

"Jeepers," Kelp said, a thing he didn't say often.

And Dire Straits wasn't even in there. They emerged on the

other side, warm, curious horse breath still moist on Dortmunder's cheek, and looked around, accustoming themselves to the darkness again. Behind them, the horses whickered and bumped around, still disturbed by this late-night visit. Far away, the main farmhouse showed just a couple of lights. Faint illumination came from window openings of nearer structures. "He has to be in that one or that one," the old coot said, pointing.

"Which one you want to try first?" Dortmunder asked.

The old coot considered and pointed. "That one."

"Then it's in the other one," Dortmunder said. "So that's where we'll try."

The old coot gave him a look. "Are you trying to be funny, or what?"

"Or what," Dortmunder said.

And, as it turned out, he was right. Third stall in on the left, there was Dire Straits himself, a big, kind of arrogant-looking thing, with a narrower-than-usual face and a very sleek black coat. He reared back and stared at these human beings with distaste, like John Barrymore being awakened the morning after. "That's him," the old coot said. More important, a small sign on the stall door said the same thing: DIRE STRAITS.

"At last," Kelp said.

"Hasn't been that long," the old coot said. "Let me get a bridle for him." He turned away, then suddenly tensed, looking back toward the door. In a quick, harsh whisper, he said, "Somebody coming!"

"Uh-oh," Dortmunder said.

Turning fast, the old coot yanked open a stall door—not the one to Dire Straits—grabbed Dortmunder's elbow in his strong, bony hand and shoved him inside, at the same time hissing at Kelp, "Slip in here! Slip in!"

"There's somebody in here," Dortmunder objected, meaning a horse, a brown one, who stared at this unexpected guest in absolute astonishment.

"No time!" The old coot was pushing Kelp in, crowding in himself, pulling the stall door shut just as the light in the barn got much brighter. Must be on a dimmer switch.

"Hey, fellas," a male voice said conversationally, "what's going on?"

Caught us, Dortmunder thought, and cast about in his mind for some even faintly sensible reason for being in this brown horse's stall in the middle of the night. Then he heard what else the voice was saying:

"Thought you were all settled down for the night."

He's talking to the horses, Dortmunder thought.

"Something get to you guys? Bird fly in?"

In a way, Dortmunder thought.

"Did a rat get in here?"

The voice was closer, calm and reassuring, its owner moving slowly along the aisle, his familiar sound and sight leaving a lot of soothed horses in his wake.

All except for the brown horse in here with Dortmunder and Kelp and the old coot. He wasn't exactly crying out, "Here, boss, here they are, they're right here!" but it was close. Snort, whuffle, paw, headshake, prance; the damn beast acted like he was auditioning for *A Chorus Line*. While Dortmunder and company crouched down low on the far side of this huge, hairy show-off, doing their best not to get crushed between the immovable object of the stall wall and the irrepressible force of the horse's haunch, the owner of the voice came over to see what was up, saying, "Hey, there, Daffy, what's the problem?"

Daffy, thought Dortmunder. I might have known.

The person was right there, leaning his forearms on the stall door, permitting Daffy to slobber and blubber all over his face. "It's OK now, Daffy," the person said. "Everything's fine."

I've been invaded! Daffy whuffled while his tail dry-mopped Dortmunder's face.

"Just settle down, big fella."

Just look me over! Have I ever had ten legs before?

"Take it easy, boy. Everybody else is calm now."

That's because they don't have these, these, these. . . .

"Good Daffy. See you in the morning."

Oh, dear, oh, dear, oh, dear, Daffy mumbled, while trying to step on everybody's toes at once.

The owner of the voice receded at last, and the old coot did something up around Daffy's head that all at once made the horse calm right down. As the lights lowered to their former dimness and the sound of thumping boots faded, Daffy grinned at everybody as though to say, *I've always wanted roommates. Nice!*

Kelp said, "What did you *do*?"

"Sugar cubes," the old coot said. "I brought some for Dire Straits, didn't have time to give one to this critter before that hand got here."

Sugar cubes. Dortmunder looked at the old coot with new respect. Here was a man who traveled with an emergency supply of sugar cubes.

"OK," the old coot said, shoving Daffy out of his way as though the animal were a big sofa on casters, "Let's get Dire Straits and get out of here."

"Exactly," Dortmunder said, but then found himself kind of pinned against the wall. "Listen, uh, Hiram," he said. "Could you move Daffy a little?"

"Oh, sure."

Hiram did, and Dortmunder gratefully left that stall, hurried along by Daffy's nose in the small of his back. Kelp shut the stall door and Hiram went over to select a bridle from among those hanging on pegs. Coming back to Dire Straits' stall, he said softly, "Come here, guy, I got something nice for you."

Dire Straits wasn't so sure about that. Being a star, he was harder to get than Daffy. From well back in the stall, he gave Hiram down his long nose a do-I-know-you? look.

"Come here, honey," Hiram urged, soft and confidential, displaying not one but two sugar cubes on his outstretched palm. "Got something for you."

Next door, Daffy stuck his head out to watch all this with some concern, having thought he had an exclusive on sugar-cube distribution. *Whicker?* he asked.

That did it. Hearing his neighbor, Dire Straits finally realized there was such a thing as playing *too* hard to get. With a toss of the head, moving with a picky-toed dignity that Dortmunder might have thought sexually suspicious if he hadn't known Dire Straits' rep, the big black beast came forward, lowered his head, wuggled and muggled over Hiram's palm and the cubes were gone. Meanwhile, with his other hand, Hiram was patting the horse's nose, murmuring, rubbing behind his ear and gradually getting into just the right position.

It was slickly done, Dortmunder had to admit that. The first thing Dire Straits knew, the bit was in his mouth, the bridle straps were around his head and Hiram was wrapping a length of rein around his own hand. "Good boy," Hiram said, gave the animal one more pat and backed away, opening the stall.

After all that prima-donna stuff, Dire Straits was suddenly no trouble at all. Maybe he thought he was on his way to the hop. As Daffy and a couple of other horses neighed goodbye, Hiram led Dire Straits out of the barn. Dortmunder and Kelp stuck close, Hiram now seeming less like an old coot and more like somebody who knew what he was doing, and they headed at an easy pace across the fields.

The fences along the way were composed of two rails, one at waist height and the other down by your knee, with their ends stuck into holes in vertical posts and nailed. On the way in, Dortmunder and Kelp had removed rails from three fences, because Hiram had assured them that Dire Straits would neither climb them nor leap over. "I thought horses jumped," Dortmunder said.

"Only jumpers," Hiram answered. Dortmunder, unsatisfied, decided to let it go.

On the way out, Hiram and Dire Straits paused while Dortmunder and Kelp restored the rails to the first fence, having to whisper harshly the length of the rail at each other before they got the damn things seated in the holes in the vertical posts, and then they moved on, Kelp muttering, "You almost took my thumb off there, you know."

"Wait till we're in the light again," Dortmunder told him. "I'll show you the big gash on the back of my hand."

"No, no, honey," Hiram said to Dire Straits. It seemed there were other horses in this field, and Dire Straits wanted to go hang out, but Hiram held tight to the rein, tugged and provided the occasional sugar cube to keep him moving in the right direction. The other horses began to come around, interested, wondering what was up. Dortmunder and Kelp did their best to keep out of the way without losing Hiram and Dire Straits, but it was getting tough. There were five or six horses milling around, bumping into one another, sticking their faces into Dortmunder's and Kelp's necks, distracting them and slowing them down. "Hey!" Dortmunder called, but softly. "Wait up!"

"We got to get out of here," Hiram said, not waiting up.

Kelp said, "Hiram, we're gonna get lost."

"Hold his tail," Hiram suggested. He still wasn't waiting up.

Dortmunder couldn't believe that. "You mean the horse?"

"Who else? He won't mind."

The sound of Hiram's voice was farther ahead. It was getting harder to tell Dire Straits from all these other beasts. "Jeez, maybe we better," Kelp said and trotted forward, arms up to protect himself from ricocheting animals.

Dortmunder followed, reluctant but seeing no other choice. He and Kelp both grabbed Dire Straits' tail, way down near the end; and from there on, the trip got somewhat easier, though it was essentially humiliating to have to walk along holding on to some horse's tail.

At the second fence, there was another batch of horses, so many that it was impossible to put the rails back. "Oh, the hell with it," Dortmunder said. "Let's just go." He grabbed Dire Straits' tail. "Come on, come on," he said, and the horse he was holding on to, which wasn't Dire Straits, suddenly took off at about 90 miles an hour, taking Dortmunder with him for the first eight inches, or until his brain could order his fingers, *"Retract!"* Reeling, not quite falling into the ooze below, Dortmunder stared around in the darkness, saying, "Where the hell *is* everybody?"

A lot of horses neighed and whickered and snorted and laughed at him; in among them all, Kelp's voice called, "Over here," and so the little band regrouped again, Dortmunder clutching firmly the right tail.

What a lot of horses—more than ever. Hiram, complaining that he didn't *have* that much sugar anymore, nevertheless occasionally had to buy off more intrusive and aggressive animals, while Dortmunder and Kelp had to keep saying, as horses stuck their noses into pants pockets and armpits, "*We* don't have the damn sugar! Talk to the guy in front!"

Finally, they reached the last fence, where Hiram suddenly stopped and said, "Oh, *hell*."

"I don't want to hear 'Oh, hell,'" Dortmunder answered. Feeling his way along Dire Straits' flank, he came up to the horse's head and saw Hiram looking at the final fence. Because this was the border of the property, on coming in Dortmunder and Kelp had left the rails roughly in their original positions, though no longer nailed in place, and now the press of horses had dislodged them, leaving a 12-foot gap full of about the biggest herd of horses this side of a Gene Autry movie. More horses joined the crowd every second, passing through the gap, disappearing into the darkness. "Now what?" Dortmunder said.

"Apples," Hiram said. He sounded unhappy.

Dortmunder said, "What apples? I don't have any apples."

"*They* do," Hiram said. "If there's one thing horses like more than sugar, it's apples. And that"—he pointed his chin in disgust—"is an orchard."

"And *that*," Kelp said, "is a siren."

It was true. Far in the distance, the wail of a siren rose and fell, and then rose again, more clearly. "Sounds exactly like the city," Dortmunder said, with a whiff of nostalgia.

Kelp said, "Aren't those lights over there? Over by the road?"

Past the bulk of many horses stretching their necks up into apple trees to eat green apples, Dortmunder saw the bobbing beams of flashlights. "Over by the van, you mean," he said. The siren rose, wonderfully distinct, then fell; and during its valley, voices could be heard, shouting, over by the flashlights. "Terrific," Dortmunder said.

"What happened," Hiram said, "is the owner. The orchard owner."

"He probably lives," Kelp suggested, "in that house we saw across the street from where we parked."

"Across the road," Hiram corrected.

"Anyway," Kelp said, "I guess he called the cops."

Beyond the bobbing flashlights, which seemed to Dortmunder to be moving closer, red and blue lights appeared, blinking and revolving. "State troopers," Dortmunder said.

"Well, we'll never get to the van," Hiram said. Turning around, looking past Dire Straits' shoulder, he said, "We can't go back that way anymore, either."

Dortmunder turned to look and saw many more lights on now in the main ranch building and the outbuildings. The ruckus over here had attracted attention, maybe; or, more likely, the owner of the orchard had phoned the owner of the ranch to say a word or two about horses eating apples.

In any event, it was a pincer movement, with the orchard people and the state troopers in front and the ranch people in back, all moving inexorably toward the point occupied by Dortmunder and Kelp and Hiram and Dire Straits.

"There's only one thing to do," Hiram said.

Dortmunder looked at him. "That many?"

"It's time to ride out of here."

Kelp said, "Hiram, we'll never get to the van."

"Not drive. *Ride.*" Saying which, Hiram suddenly swung up onto Dire Straits' bare back. The horse looked startled, and maybe insulted. "Grab mounts," Hiram said, gripping the rein.

"Hiram," Dortmunder said, "I don't ride horses."

"Time to learn, Bo," Hiram said unsympathetically. Bending low over Dire Straits' neck, whamming his heels into Dire Straits' rib cage, Hiram yelled into Dire Straits' ear, "*Go,* boy!"

"I don't *ride,*" Dortmunder said, "any *horses.*"

With Hiram on his back, Dire Straits walked over to the nearest apple tree and started to eat. "*Go,* boy!" Hiram yelled, kicking and whacking the oblivious thoroughbred. "Giddy*ap,* damn it!" he yelled, as flashlight beams began to pick him out among the branches and leaves and green apples.

"I never did have much luck with horses," Dortmunder said. Out in front of him was a scene of mass, and growing, confusion. As the siren's wail continued to weave, horses shouldered their way up and down the tight rows of gnarly apple trees, munching and socializing. Human beings uselessly yelled and waved things among them, trying to make them go home. Because green apples go right through horses, the human beings also slipped and slued a lot. Hiram, trying to hide in the tree Dire Straits was snacking off but blinded by all the flashlights now converged on him, fell out of the tree and into the arms of what looked very much like a state trooper, who then fell down. Other people fell down. Horses ate. Lights stabbed this way and that. Back by the

breached fence, Dortmunder and Kelp watched without pleasure. "That reminds me of the subway," Dortmunder said.

"Here comes that truck," Kelp said.

Dortmunder turned, and here came a pair of headlights
through the night from the ranch, jouncing up and down. "I do
understand pickup trucks," Dortmunder said and strode toward
the lights.

Kelp, saying, "John? You got something?" came trailing along.

Dortmunder and the pickup approached each other. As the
vehicle neared, Dortmunder waved his arms over his head, de-
manding that the thing stop, which it did, and a sleepy young
guy looked out at him, saying, "Who the hell are you?"

"Your goddamn horses," Dortmunder said, his manner outraged but disciplined, "are eating our goddamn apples."

The fellow stared at him. "You aren't Russwinder."

"I *work* for him, don't I?" Dortmunder demanded. "And I
never *seen* anybody so mad. We need light back there, he sent us
down, get your portable generator. You *got* a portable generator,
don't you?"

"Well, sure," the fellow said. "But I was gonna—"

"*Light,*" Dortmunder insisted. Around them, half-awake and
half-dressed ranch employees made their way toward the center
of chaos, ignoring Dortmunder and Kelp, whose bona fides were
established by their being in conversation with the ranch's
pickup truck. "We can't see what we're doing back there," Dortmunder said, "and Mr. Russwinder's *mad.*"

The young fellow clearly saw that this was a time to be accommodating to one's neighbor and to one's neighbor's employee. "OK," he said. "Climb in."

"We'll ride in back," Dortmunder told him and clambered up
into the bed of the pickup, which was pleasantly aromatic of hay.
Kelp followed, eyes bright with hope, and the pickup lurched forward, jounced around in a great circle and headed back toward
the ranch.

The pickup seemed to think *it* was a horse; over the fields it bucked and bounced, like a frying pan trying to throw Dortmunder and Kelp back into the fire. Clutching the pickup's metal parts with every finger and every toe, Dortmunder gazed back at the receding scene in the orchard, which looked now like a battle in a movie about the Middle Ages. "Never again," he said.

Ka-*bump*! The pickup slued from field to dirt road, a much more user-friendly surface, and hustled off toward the barns. "Well, this time," Kelp said, "you can't blame me."

Dortmunder looked at him. "Why not?"

The cowboy behind the wheel slammed both feet and a brick onto the brake pedal, causing the pickup to skid halfway around, hurl itself broadside at the brown-plank wall of the nearest barn and shudder to a stop with millimeters to spare. Dortmunder peeled himself off the pickup's bed, staring wildly around, and the maniac driver hopped out, crying, "The generator's in here!" Off he went at a lope.

Dortmunder and Kelp shakily assisted each other to the ground, as their benefactor dashed into the barn. "I'd like to wait and run him over," Dortmunder said, getting into the pickup's cab and sliding over to the passenger side.

Kelp followed, settling behind the wheel. The engine was on, so he just shifted into gear and they drove away from there, brisk but not reckless. No need to be reckless.

At the highway, Dortmunder said, "Left leads past that orchard. Better go right, up the hill."

So they went up the hill. As they drove past the high clearing where they'd taken pictures down at the ranch, Kelp slowed and said, "Look at that!"

It was positively coruscating down there, dazzling, like night-time on the Fourth of July. Police and fire engine flashing lights in red and blue mingled with the white of headlights, flashlights, spotlights. Men and horses ran hither and yon. Every building in the area was all lit up.

"Just for a second," Kelp said, pulling off the road and coming to a stop.

Dortmunder didn't argue. It was really a very interesting sight, and they could, after all, claim some part in its creation. They got out and walked to the edge of the drop-off to watch. Faint cries and horse snorts drifted up through the sultry air.

"We better go," Dortmunder said at last.

"Ya. You're right."

They turned back to the pickup, and Kelp said, with surprise, "Well, look at this!" He reached out his hand and took the end of a bridle and turned to smile at Dortmunder, saying, "I guess he likes us!"

Dortmunder looked at the creature munching calmly at the other end of the bridle. "It *is* him, isn't it?"

"He followed me home," Kelp said, grinning broadly. "Can I keep him?"

"No," Dortmunder said.

Surprised, Kelp ducked his head and hissed, so Dire Straits wouldn't hear him, "Dortmunder, the insurance company! A million dollars!"

"I am not taking a stolen race horse through the Lincoln Tunnel," Dortmunder said. "That's just for openers. And we got no place to keep him."

"In the park."

"He'd get mugged. He'd get stolen. He'd get found."

"We gotta know somebody with a back yard!"

"And neighbors. Andy, it doesn't play. Now, come on, say goodbye to your friend; we're going home."

Dortmunder continued on to the pickup, but Kelp stayed where he was, an agonized expression on his face. When Dortmunder looked back, Kelp said, "I can't, John, I just can't." The hand clutching the bridle shook. "I'm holding a million dollars! I can't let go."

Dortmunder got into the pickup, behind the wheel. He looked out through the open passenger door at Kelp in the dark, on the hilltop, holding a strip of leather with $1,000,000 on the other end. "I'm going to New York now," Dortmunder told him, not unkindly. "Are you coming, or are you staying?"

TOO MANY CROOKS

"DID YOU HEAR SOMETHING?" DORTMUNDER WHISPERED.

"The wind," Kelp said.

Dortmunder twisted around in his seated position and deliberately shone the flashlight in the kneeling Kelp's eyes. "What wind? We're in a tunnel."

"There's underground rivers," Kelp said, squinting, "so maybe there's underground winds. Are you through the wall there?"

"Two more whacks," Dortmunder told him. Relenting, he aimed the flashlight past Kelp back down the empty tunnel, a meandering, messy gullet, most of it less than three feet in diameter, wriggling its way through rocks and rubble and ancient middens, traversing 40 tough feet from the rear of the basement of the out-of-business shoe store to the wall of the bank on the corner. According to the maps Dortmunder had gotten from the water department by claiming to be with the sewer department, and the maps he'd gotten from the sewer department by claiming to be with the water department, just the other side of this wall was the bank's main vault. Two more whacks and this large, irregular square of concrete that Dortmunder and Kelp had been scoring and scratching at for some time now would at last fall away onto the floor inside, and there would be the vault.

Dortmunder gave it a whack.

Dortmunder gave it another whack.

The block of concrete fell onto the floor of the vault. "Oh, thank God," somebody said.

What? Reluctant but unable to stop himself, Dortmunder dropped sledge and flashlight and leaned his head through the hole in the wall and looked around.

It was the vault, all right. And it was full of people.

A man in a suit stuck his hand out and grabbed Dortmunder's and shook it while pulling him through the hole and on into the vault. "Great work, Officer," he said. "The robbers are outside."

Dortmunder had thought he and Kelp were the robbers. "They are?"

A round-faced woman in pants and a Buster Brown collar said, "Five of them. With machine guns."

"Machine guns," Dortmunder said.

A delivery kid wearing a mustache and an apron and carrying a flat cardboard carton containing four coffees, two decafs and a tea said, "We all hostages, mon. I gonna get fired."

"How many of you are there?" the man in the suit asked, looking past Dortmunder at Kelp's nervously smiling face.

"Just the two," Dortmunder said, and watched helplessly as willing hands dragged Kelp through the hole and set him on his feet in the vault. It was really very full of hostages.

"I'm Kearney," the man in the suit said. "I'm the bank manager, and I can't tell you how glad I am to see you."

Which was the first time any bank manager had said *that* to Dortmunder, who said, "Uh-huh, uh-huh," and nodded, and then said, "I'm, uh, Officer Diddums, and this is Officer, uh, Kelly."

Kearney, the bank manager, frowned. "Diddums, did you say?"

Dortmunder was furious with himself. Why did I call myself Diddums? Well, I didn't know I was going to need an alias inside a bank vault, did I? Aloud, he said, "Uh-huh. Diddums. It's Welsh."

"Ah," said Kearney. Then he frowned again and said, "You people aren't even armed."

"Well, no," Dortmunder said. "We're the, uh, the hostage-rescue team; we don't want any shots fired, increase the risk for you, uh, civilians."

"Very shrewd," Kearney agreed.

Kelp, his eyes kind of glassy and his smile kind of fixed, said, "Well, folks, maybe we should leave here now, single file, just make your way in an orderly fashion through—"

"They're coming!" hissed a stylish woman over by the vault door.

Everybody moved. It was amazing; everybody shifted at once. Some people moved to hide the new hole in the wall, some people moved to get farther away from the vault door and some people moved to get behind Dortmunder, who suddenly found himself the nearest person in the vault to that big, round, heavy metal door, which was easing massively and silently open.

It stopped halfway, and three men came in. They wore black ski masks and black leather jackets and black work pants and black shoes. They carried Uzi submachine guns at high port. Their eyes looked cold and hard, and their hands fidgeted on the metal of the guns, and their feet danced nervously, even when they were standing still. They looked as though anything at all might make them overreact.

"Shut up!" one of them yelled, though nobody'd been talking. He glared around at his guests and said, "Gotta have somebody to stand out front, see can the cops be trusted." His eye, as Dortmunder had known it would, lit on Dortmunder. "You," he said.

"Uh-huh," Dortmunder said.

"What's your name?"

Everybody in the vault had already heard him say it, so what choice did he have? "Diddums," Dortmunder said.

The robber glared at Dortmunder through his ski mask. "Diddums?"

"It's Welsh," Dortmunder explained.

"Ah," the robber said, and nodded. He gestured with the Uzi. "Outside, Diddums."

Dortmunder stepped forward, glancing back over his shoulder at all the people looking at him, knowing every goddamn one of them was glad he wasn't him—even Kelp, back there pretending to be four feet tall—and then Dortmunder stepped through the vault door, surrounded by all those nervous maniacs with machine guns, and went with them down a corridor flanked by desks and through a doorway to the main part of the bank, which was a mess.

The time at the moment, as the clock high on the wide wall confirmed, was 5:15 in the afternoon. Everybody who worked at the bank should have gone home by now; that was the theory Dortmunder had been operating from. What must have happened was, just before closing time at three o'clock (Dortmunder and Kelp being already then in the tunnel, working hard, knowing nothing of events on the surface of the planet), these gaudy showboats had come into the bank waving their machine guns around.

And not just waving them, either. Lines of ragged punctures had been drawn across the walls and the Lucite upper panel of the tellers' counter, like connect-the-dot puzzles. Wastebaskets and a potted Ficus had been overturned, but fortunately, there were no bodies lying around; none Dortmunder could see, anyway. The big plate-glass front windows had been shot out, and two more of the black-clad robbers were crouched down, one behind the OUR LOW LOAN RATES poster and the other behind the OUR HIGH IRA RATES poster, staring out at the street, from which came the sound of somebody talking loudly but indistinctly through a bullhorn.

So what must have happened, they'd come in just before three, waving their guns, figuring a quick in and out, and some brown-nose employee looking for advancement triggered the alarm, and now they had a stalemate hostage situation on their hands; and, of course, everybody in the world by now has seen *Dog Day After-noon* and therefore knows that if the police get the drop on a rob-ber in circumstances such as these circumstances right here, they'll immediately shoot him dead, so now hostage negotiation is trickier than ever. This isn't what I had in mind when I came to the bank, Dortmunder thought.

The boss robber prodded him along with the barrel of his Uzi, saying, "What's your first name, Diddums?"

Please don't say Dan, Dortmunder begged himself. Please, please, somehow, anyhow, manage not to say Dan. His mouth opened, "John," he heard himself say, his brain having turned desperately in this emergency to that last resort, the truth, and he got weak-kneed with relief.

"OK, John, don't faint on me," the robber said. "This is very simple what you got to do here. The cops say they want to talk, just talk, nobody gets hurt. Fine. So you're gonna step out in front of the bank and see do the cops shoot you."

"Ah," Dortmunder said.

"No time like the present, huh, John?" the robber said, and poked him with the Uzi again.

"That kind of hurts," Dortmunder said.

"I apologize," the robber said, hard-eyed. "Out."

One of the other robbers, eyes red with strain inside the black ski mask, leaned close to Dortmunder and yelled, "You wanna shot in the foot first? You wanna *crawl* out there?"

"I'm going," Dortmunder told him. "See? Here I go."

The first robber, the comparatively calm one, said, "You go as far as the sidewalk, that's all. You take one step off the curb, we blow your head off."

"Got it," Dortmunder assured him, and crunched across bro-ken glass to the sagging-open door and looked out. Across the street was parked a line of buses, police cars, police trucks, all in blue and white with red gumdrops on top, and behind them moved a seething mass of armed cops. "Uh," Dortmunder said.

Turning back to the comparatively calm robber, he said, "You wouldn't happen to have a white flag or anything like that, would you?"

The robber pressed the point of the Uzi to Dortmunder's side. "Out," he said.

"Right," Dortmunder said. He faced front, put his hands way up in the air and stepped outside.

What a *lot* of attention he got. From behind all those blue-and-whites on the other side of the street, tense faces stared. On the rooftops of the red-brick tenements, in this neighborhood deep in the residential heart of Queens, sharpshooters began to familiarize themselves through their telescopic sights with the contours of Dortmunder's furrowed brow. To left and right, the ends of the block were sealed off with buses parked nose to tailpipe, past which ambulances and jumpy white-coated medics could be seen. Everywhere, rifles and pistols jittered in nervous fingers. Adrenaline ran in the gutters.

"I'm not with *them*!" Dortmunder shouted, edging across the sidewalk, arms upraised, hoping this announcement wouldn't upset the other bunch of armed hysterics behind him. For all he knew, they had a problem with rejection.

However, nothing happened behind him, and what happened out front was that a bullhorn appeared, resting on a police-car roof, and roared at him, "*You a hostage?*"

"I sure am!" yelled Dortmunder.

"*What's your name?*"

Oh, not again, thought Dortmunder, but there was nothing for it. "Diddums," he said.

"*What?*"

"*Diddums!*"

A brief pause: "*Diddums?*"

"*It's Welsh!*"

"Ah."

There was a little pause while whoever was operating the bullhorn conferred with his compatriots, and then the bullhorn said, *"What's the situation in there?"*

What kind of question was that? "Well, uh," Dortmunder said, and remembered to speak more loudly, and called, "kind of tense, actually."

"Any of the hostages been harmed?"

"Uh-uh. No. Definitely not. This is a . . . this is a . . . nonviolent confrontation." Dortmunder fervently hoped to establish that idea in everybody's mind, particularly if he were going to be out here in the middle much longer.

"Any change in the situation?"

Change? "Well," Dortmunder answered, "I haven't been in there that long, but it seems like—"

"Not that long? What's the matter with you, Diddums? You've been in that bank over two hours now!"

"Oh, yeah!" Forgetting, Dortmunder lowered his arms and stepped forward to the curb. "That's right!" he called. "Two hours! *More* than two hours! Been in there a long time!"

"Step out here away from the bank!"

Dortmunder looked down and saw his toes hanging ten over the edge of the curb. Stepping back at a brisk pace, he called, "I'm not supposed to do that!"

"Listen, Diddums, I've got a lot of tense men and women over here. I'm telling you, step away from the bank!"

"The fellas inside," Dortmunder explained, "they don't want me to step off the curb. They said they'd, uh, well, they just don't want me to do it."

"Psst! Hey, Diddums!"

Dortmunder paid no attention to the voice calling from behind him. He was concentrating too hard on what was happening right now out front. Also, he wasn't that used to the new name yet.

"Diddums!"

"Maybe you better put your hands up again."

"Oh, yeah!" Dortmunder's arms shot up like pistons blowing through an engine block. "There they are!"

"Diddums, goddamn it, do I have to *shoot* you to get you to pay attention?"

Arms dropping, Dortmunder spun around. "Sorry! I wasn't— I was— Here I am!"

"Get those goddamn hands up!"

Dortmunder turned sideways, arms up so high his sides hurt. Peering sidelong to his right, he called to the crowd across the street, "Sirs, they're talking to me inside now." Then he peered sidelong to his left, saw the comparatively calm robber crouched beside the broken doorframe and looking less calm than before, and he said, "Here I am."

"We're gonna give them our demands now," the robber said. "Through you."

"That's fine," Dortmunder said. "That's great. Only, you know, how come you don't do it on the phone? I mean, the way it's normally—"

The red-eyed robber, heedless of exposure to the sharpshooters across the street, shouldered furiously past the comparatively calm robber, who tried to restrain him as he yelled at Dortmunder, "You're rubbing it in, are ya? OK, I made a mistake! I got excited and I shot up the switchboard! You want me to get excited again?"

"No, no!" Dortmunder cried, trying to hold his hands straight up in the air and defensively in front of his body at the same time. "I forgot! I just forgot!"

The other robbers all clustered around to grab the red-eyed robber, who seemed to be trying to point his Uzi in Dortmunder's direction as he yelled, "I did it in front of everybody! I humiliated myself in front of everybody! And now you're making fun of me!"

"I *forgot*! I'm sorry!"

"You can't forget that! Nobody's ever gonna forget that!"

The three remaining robbers dragged the red-eyed robber back away from the doorway, talking to him, trying to soothe him, leaving Dortmunder and the comparatively calm robber to continue their conversation. "I'm sorry," Dortmunder said. "I just forgot. I've been kind of distracted lately. Recently."

"You're playing with fire here, Diddums," the robber said. "Now tell them they're gonna get our demands."

Dortmunder nodded, and turned his head the other way, and yelled, "They're gonna tell you their demands now. I mean, *I'm* gonna tell you their demands. *Their* demands. Not *my* demands. *Their* de—"

"We're willing to listen, Diddums, only so long as none of the hostages get hurt."

"That's good!" Dortmunder agreed, and turned his head the other way to tell the robber, "That's reasonable, you know, that's sensible, that's a very good thing they're saying."

"Shut up," the robber said.

"Right," Dortmunder said.

The robber said, "First, we want the riflemen off the roofs."

"Oh, so do I," Dortmunder told him, and turned to shout, "They want the riflemen off the roofs!"

"What else?"

"What else?"

"And we want them to unblock that end of the street, the— what is it?—the north end."

Dortmunder frowned straight ahead at the buses blocking the intersection. "Isn't that east?" he asked.

"Whatever it is," the robber said, getting impatient. "That end down there to the left."

"OK." Dortmunder turned his head and yelled, "They want you to unblock the east end of the street!" Since his hands were way up in the sky somewhere, he pointed with his chin.

"Isn't that north?"

"I knew it was," the robber said.

"Yeah, I guess so," Dortmunder called. "That end down there to the left."

"The right, you mean."

"Yeah, that's right. Your right, my left. *Their* left."

"What else?"

Dortmunder sighed, and turned his head. "What else?"

The robber glared at him. "I can *hear* the bullhorn, Diddums. I can *hear* him say 'What else?' You don't have to repeat everything he says. No more translations."

"Right," Dortmunder said. "Gotcha. No more translations."

"We'll want a car," the robber told him. "A station wagon. We're gonna take three hostages with us, so we want a big station wagon. And nobody follows us."

"Gee," Dortmunder said dubiously, "are you sure?"

The robber stared. "Am I *sure?*"

"Well, you know what they'll do," Dortmunder told him, lowering his voice so the other team across the street couldn't hear him. "What they do in these situations, they fix a little radio transmitter under the car, so then they don't have to *follow* you, exactly, but they know where you are."

Impatient again, the robber said, "So you'll tell them not to do that. No radio transmitters, or we kill the hostages."

"Well, I suppose," Dortmunder said doubtfully.

"What's wrong *now?*" the robber demanded. "You're too goddamn *picky,* Diddums; you're just the messenger here. You think you know my job better than I do?"

I know I do, Dortmunder thought, but it didn't seem a judicious thing to say aloud, so instead, he explained, "I just want things to go smooth, that's all. I just don't want bloodshed. And I was thinking, the New York City police, you know, well, they've got helicopters."

"Damn," the robber said. He crouched low to the littered floor, behind the broken doorframe, and brooded about his situation. Then he looked up at Dortmunder and said, "OK, Diddums, you're so smart. What *should* we do?"

Dortmunder blinked. "You want *me* to figure out your get-away?"

"Put yourself in our position," the robber suggested. "Think about it."

Dortmunder nodded. Hands in the air, he gazed at the blocked intersection and put himself in the robbers' position. "Hoo, boy," he said. "You're in a real mess."

"We *know* that, Diddums."

"Well," Dortmunder said, "I tell you what maybe you could do. You make them give you one of those buses they've got down there blocking the street. They give you one of those buses right now, then you know they haven't had time to put anything cute in it, like time-release tear-gas grenades or anyth—"

"Oh, my God," the robber said. His black ski mask seemed to have paled slightly.

"Then you take *all* the hostages," Dortmunder told him. "Everybody goes in the bus, and one of you people drives, and you go somewhere real crowded, like Times Square, say, and then you stop and make all the hostages get out and run."

"Yeah?" the robber said. "What good does that do us?"

"Well," Dortmunder said, "you drop the ski masks and the leather jackets and the guns, and *you* run, too. Twenty, thirty people all running away from the bus in different directions, in the middle of Times Square in rush hour, everybody losing themselves in the crowd. It might work."

"Jeez, it might," the robber said. "OK, go ahead and— What?"

"What?" Dortmunder echoed. He strained to look leftward, past the vertical column of his left arm. The boss robber was in excited conversation with one of his pals; not the red-eyed maniac, a different one. The boss robber shook his head and said, "Damn!" Then he looked up at Dortmunder. "Come back in here, Diddums," he said.

Dortmunder said, "But don't you want me to—"

"Come back in here!"

"Oh," Dortmunder said. "Uh, I better tell them over there that I'm gonna move."

"Make it fast," the robber told him. "Don't mess with me, Diddums. I'm in a bad mood right now."

"OK." Turning his head the other way, hating it that his back was toward this bad-mooded robber for even a second, Dortmunder called, "They want me to go back into the bank now. Just for a minute." Hands still up, he edged sideways across the sidewalk and through the gaping doorway, where the robbers laid hands on him and flung him back deeper into the bank.

He nearly lost his balance but saved himself against the sideways-lying pot of the tipped-over Ficus. When he turned around, all five of the robbers were lined up looking at him, their expressions intent, focused, almost hungry, like a row of cats looking in a fish-store window. "Uh," Dortmunder said.

"He's it now," one of the robbers said.

Another robber said, "But *they* don't know it."

A third robber said, "They will soon."

"They'll know it when nobody gets on the bus," the boss robber said, and shook his head at Dortmunder. "Sorry, Diddums. Your idea doesn't work anymore."

Dortmunder had to keep reminding himself that he wasn't actually *part* of this string. "How come?" he asked.

Disgusted, one of the other robbers said, "The rest of the hostages got away, that's how come."

Wide-eyed, Dortmunder spoke without thinking: "The tunnel!"

All of a sudden, it got very quiet in the bank. The robbers were now looking at him like cats looking at a fish with no window in the way. "The tunnel?" repeated the boss robber slowly. "You *know* about the tunnel?"

"Well, kind of," Dortmunder admitted. "I mean, the guys digging it, they got there just before you came and took me away."

"And you never mentioned it."

"Well," Dortmunder said, very uncomfortable, "I didn't feel like I should."

The red-eyed maniac lunged forward, waving that submachine gun again, yelling, "*You're* the guy with the tunnel! It's your tunnel!" And he pointed the shaking barrel of the Uzi at Dortmunder's nose.

"Easy, easy!" the boss robber yelled. "This is our only hostage; don't use him up!"

The red-eyed maniac reluctantly lowered the Uzi, but he turned to the others and announced, "*Nobody's* gonna forget when I shot up the switchboard. Nobody's *ever* gonna forget that. He wasn't *here*!"

All of the robbers thought that over. Meantime, Dortmunder was thinking about his own position. He might be a hostage, but he wasn't your normal hostage, because he was also a guy who had just dug a tunnel to a bank vault, and there were maybe 30 eyeball witnesses who could identify him. So it wasn't enough to get away from these bank robbers; he was also going to have to get away from the police. Several thousand police.

So did that mean he was locked to these second-rate smash-and-grabbers? Was his own future really dependent on *their* getting out of this hole? Bad news, if true. Left to their own devices, these people couldn't escape from a merry-go-round.

Dortmunder sighed. "OK," he said. "The first thing we have to do is—"

"We?" the boss robber said. "Since when are you in this?"

"Since you dragged me in," Dortmunder told him. "And the first thing we have to do is—"

The red-eyed maniac lunged at him again with the Uzi, shouting, "Don't you tell us what to do! We know what to do!"

"I'm your only hostage," Dortmunder reminded him. "Don't use me up. Also, now that I've seen you people in action, I'm your only hope of getting out of here. So this time, listen to me. The first thing we have to do is close and lock the vault door."

One of the robbers gave a scornful laugh. "The hostages are *gone,*" he said. "Didn't you hear that part? Lock the vault door after the hostages are gone. Isn't that some kind of old saying?" And he laughed and laughed.

Dortmunder looked at him. "It's a two-way tunnel," he said quietly.

The robbers stared at him. Then they all turned and ran toward the back of the bank. They *all* did.

They're too excitable for this line of work, Dortmunder thought as he walked briskly toward the front of the bank. *Clang* went the vault door, far behind him, and Dortmunder stepped through the broken doorway and out again to the sidewalk, remembering to stick his arms straight up in the air as he did.

"Hi!" he yelled, sticking his face well out, displaying it for all the sharpshooters to get a really *good* look at. "Hi, it's me again! Diddums! Welsh!"

"Diddums!" screamed an enraged voice from deep within the bank. "Come back here!"

Oh, no. Ignoring that, moving steadily but without panic, arms up, face forward, eyes wide, Dortmunder angled leftward across the sidewalk, shouting, "I'm coming out again! And I'm *escaping!*" And he dropped his arms, tucked his elbows in and ran hell for leather toward those blocking buses.

Gunfire encouraged him: a sudden burst behind him of *ddrrritt, ddrrritt,* and then *kopp-kopp-kopp,* and then a whole symphony of *fooms* and *thug-thugs* and *padapows.* Dortmunder's toes, turning into high-tension steel springs, kept him bounding through the air like the Wright brothers' first airplane, swooping and plunging down the middle of the street, that wall of buses getting closer and closer.

"Here! In here!" Uniformed cops appeared on both sidewalks, waving to him, offering sanctuary in the forms of open doorways and police vehicles to crouch behind, but Dortmunder was *escaping.* From everything.

The buses. He launched himself through the air, hit the black-top hard and rolled under the nearest bus. Roll, roll, roll, hitting his head and elbows and knees and ears and nose and various other parts of his body against any number of hard, dirty objects, and then he was past the bus and on his feet, staggering, staring at a lot of goggle-eyed medics hanging around beside their ambulances, who just stood there and gawked back.

Dortmunder turned left. *Medics* weren't going to chase him; their franchise didn't include healthy bodies running down the street. The cops couldn't chase him until they'd moved their buses out of the way. Dortmunder took off like the last of the dodoes, flapping his arms, wishing he knew how to fly.

The out-of-business shoe store, the other terminus of the tunnel, passed on his left. The getaway car they'd parked in front of it was long gone, of course. Dortmunder kept thudding on, on, on.

Three blocks later, a gypsy cab committed a crime by picking him up even though he hadn't phoned the dispatcher first; in the city of New York, only licensed medallion taxis are permitted to pick up customers who hail them on the street. Dortmunder, panting like a Saint Bernard on the lumpy back seat, decided not to turn the guy in.

His faithful companion May came out of the living room when Dortmunder opened the front door of his apartment and stepped into his hall. "*There* you are!" she said. "Thank goodness. It's all over the radio *and* the television."

"I may never leave the house again," Dortmunder told her. "If Andy Kelp ever calls, says he's got this great job, easy, piece of cake, I'll just tell him I've retired."

"Andy's here," May said. "In the living room. You want a beer?"

"Yes," Dortmunder said simply.

May went away to the kitchen and Dortmunder limped into

the living room, where Kelp was seated on the sofa holding a can of beer and looking happy. On the coffee table in front of him was a mountain of money.

Dortmunder stared. "What's *that*?"

Kelp grinned and shook his head. "It's been too long since we scored, John," he said. "You don't even recognize the stuff anymore. This is money."

"But— From the vault? How?"

"After you were taken away by those other guys—they were caught, by the way," Kelp interrupted himself, "without loss of life—anyway, I told everybody in the vault there, the way to keep the money safe from the robbers was we'd all carry it out with us. So we did. And then I decided what we should do is put it all in the trunk of my unmarked police car in front of the shoe store, so I could drive it to the precinct for safekeeping while they all went home to rest from their ordeal."

Dortmunder looked at his friend. He said, "You got the hostages to carry the money from the vault."

"And put it in our car," Kelp said. "Yeah, that's what I did."

May came in and handed Dortmunder a beer. He drank deep, and Kelp said, "They're looking for you, of course. Under that other name."

May said, "That's the one thing I don't understand. Diddums?"

"It's Welsh," Dortmunder told her. Then he smiled upon the mountain of money on the coffee table. "It's not a bad name," he decided. "I may keep it."

A MIDSUMMER DAYDREAM

IT HAVING BECOME ADVISABLE TO LEAVE NEW YORK CITY FOR AN indefinite period, Dortmunder and Kelp found themselves in the countryside, in a barn, watching a lot of fairies dance. "I don't know about this," Dortmunder muttered.

"It's perfect cover," Kelp whispered. "Who'd look for us *here*?"

"*I* wouldn't, that's for sure."

The fairies all skipped off stage and some other people came on and went off, and then the audience stood up. "That's it?" Dortmunder asked. "We can go now?"

"First half," Kelp told him.

First half. Near the end of the first half, one of the players in bib overalls had gone out and come back in with a donkey's head on, which about summed up Dortmunder's attitude toward the whole thing. Oh, well; when in Rome, do as the Romans, and when in West Urbino, New York, go to the Saturday-afternoon summer theater. Why not? But he wouldn't come back Sunday.

Outside, the audience stood around in the sunshine and talked about everything except *A Midsummer Night's Dream*. The women discussed other women's clothing and the men brought one another up to date on sports and the prices of automobiles, all except Kelp's cousin, a stout man named Jesse Bohker, who smelled of fertilizer because that's what he sold for a living, and who talked about the size of the audience because he was the chief investor in this barn converted to an extremely barnlike summer theater, with splintery bleachers and nonunion actors up from New York. "Good gate," Bohker said, nodding at the crowd in satisfaction, showbiz jargon as comfortable as a hay stalk in his mouth. "Shakespeare brings 'em in every time. They don't want anybody to think they don't have culture."

"Isn't that great," Kelp said, working on his enthusiasm because his cousin Bohker was putting them up until New York became a little less fraught. "Only eighty miles from the city, and you've got live theater."

"Cable kills us at night," cousin Bohker said, sharing more of his entertainment-world expertise, "but in the daytime, we do fine."

They rang a cowbell to announce the second half, and the audience obediently shuffled back in, as though they had bells round their own necks. All except Dortmunder, who said, "I don't think I can do it."

"Come *on*, John," Kelp said, not wanting to be rude to the cousin. "Don't you wanna know how it comes out?"

"I know how it comes out," Dortmunder said. "The guy with the donkey head turns into Pinocchio."

"That's OK, Andy," cousin Bohker said. He was a magnanimous host. "Some people just don't go for it," he went on, with the fat chuckle that served him so well in fertilizer sales. "Tell the truth, football season, I wouldn't go for it myself."

"I'll be out here," Dortmunder said. "In the air."

So everybody else shuffled back into the barn and Dortmunder stayed outside, like the last smoker in the world. He walked around a bit, looking at how dusty his shoes were getting, and thought about New York. It was just a little misunderstanding down there, that's all, a little question about the value of the contents of trucks that had been taken from Greenwich Street out to Long Island City one night when their regular drivers were asleep in bed. It would straighten itself out eventually, but a couple of the people involved were a little jumpy and emotional in their responses, and Dortmunder didn't want to be the cause of their having performed actions they would later regret. So it was better—more healthful, in fact—to spend a little time in the country, with the air and the trees and the sun and the fairies in the bottom of the barn.

Laughter inside the barn. Dortmunder wandered over to the main entrance, which now stood unguarded, the former ushers and cashier all away being fairies, and beyond the bleachers, he saw the guy in the donkey head and the girl dressed in curtains carrying on as before. No change. Dortmunder turned away and made a long, slow circuit of the barn, just for something to do.

This used to be a real farm a long time ago, but most of the land was sold off and a couple of outbuildings underwent insurance fires, so now the property was pretty much just the old white farmhouse, the red barn and the gravel parking lot in between. The summer-theater people were living in the farmhouse, which meant that, out back, it had the most colorful clothesline in the county. Down the road that-a-way was West Urbino proper, where cousin Bohker's big house stood.

The second half took a long time, almost as long as if Dortmunder had been inside watching it. He walked around awhile, and then he chose a comfortable-looking car in the parking lot and sat in it—people didn't lock their cars or their houses or anything around here—and then he strolled around some more, and that's when the actor with the donkey's head and the bib overalls went by, maybe to make an entrance from the front of the theater. Dortmunder nodded his head at the guy, and the actor nodded his donkey head back.

Dortmunder strolled through the parked cars, wondering if there were time to take one for a little spin, and then Mr. Donkey came back again and they both did their head nod, and the donkey walked on, and that was it for excitement. Dortmunder figured he probably *didn't* have time to take a little drive around the countryside particularly because, dollars to doughnuts, he'd get lost.

And it was a good thing he'd decided not to leave, because only about ten minutes later, a whole lot of applause sounded inside the barn and a couple of ex-fairies came trotting out to be traffic control in the parking lot. Dortmunder swam upstream through the sated culture lovers and found Kelp to one side of the flow, near the cashier's makeshift office, waiting for cousin Bohker to quit drooling over the take. "It was a lot of fun," Kelp said.

"Good."

"And it come out completely different from what you said."

Cousin Bohker emerged from the ticket office with a brand-new expression on his face, all pinched-in and pruny, as though he'd been eating his fertilizer. He said, "Andy, I guess your friend doesn't understand much about country hospitality."

This made very little sense at all; in fact, none. Kelp said, "Come again, cuz?"

"So you talk to him, Andy," cousin Bohker said. He wasn't looking at Dortmunder, but his head seemed to incline slightly in Dortmunder's direction. He seemed like a man torn between anger and fear, anger forbidding him to show the fear, fear holding the anger in check; constipated, in other words. "You talk to your *friend*," cousin Bohker said in a strangled way, "you explain about hospitality in the country, and you tell him we'll forget—"

"If you mean, John," Kelp said, "he's right here. This is him here."

"That's OK," the cousin said. "You just tell him we'll forget all about it this once, and all he has to do is give it back, and we'll never say another word about it."

Kelp shook his head. "I don't get what you mean," he said. "Give *what* back?"

"The receipts!" cousin Bohker yelled, waving madly at his ticket office. "Two hundred twenty-seven paid admissions, not counting freebies and house seats like *you* fellas had, at twelve bucks a head; that's two thousand, seven hundred twenty-four dollars, and I want it *back*!"

Kelp stared at his cousin. "The *box*-office receipts? You can't—" His stare, disbelieving, doubtful, wondering, turned toward Dortmunder. "John? You didn't!" Kelp's eyes looked like hubcaps. "Did you? You didn't! Naturally, you didn't. Did you?"

The experience of being unjustly accused was so novel and bewildering to Dortmunder that he was almost drunk from it. He had so little experience of innocence. How does an innocent person act, react, respond to the base accusation? He could barely stand up, he was concentrating so hard on this sudden in-rush of guiltlessness. His knees were wobbling. He stared at Andy Kelp and couldn't think of one solitary thing to say.

"Who else was out here?" the cousin demanded. "All alone out here while everybody else was inside with the play. 'Couldn't stand Shakespeare,' was that it? Saw his opportunity, by God, and *took* it, and the hell with his host!"

Kelp was beginning to look desperate. "John," he said, like a lawyer leading a particularly stupid witness, "you weren't just playing a little *joke*, were you? Just having a little fun, didn't mean anything serious, was that it?"

Maybe innocent people are dignified, Dortmunder thought. He tried it: "I did not take the money," he said, as dignified as a turkey on Thanksgiving eve.

Kelp turned to his cousin: "Are you *sure* it's gone?"

"Andy," said the cousin, drawing himself up—or in—becoming even more dignified than Dortmunder, topping Dortmunder's king of dignity with his own ace, "this fellow is what he is, but you're my wife's blood relative."

"Aw, cuz," Kelp protested, "you don't think I was *in* it with him, do you?"

And that was the unkindest cut of all. Forgetting dignity,

Dortmunder gazed on his former friend like a betrayed beagle. "You, too, Andy?"

"Gee whiz, John," Kelp said, twisting back and forth to show how conflicted all this made him, "what're we supposed to *think*? I mean, maybe it just happened accidental-like; you were bored, you know, walking around, you just picked up this cash without even thinking about it, you could. . . ."

Wordlessly, Dortmunder frisked himself, patting his pockets and chest, then spreading his arms wide, offering himself for Kelp to search.

Which Kelp didn't want to do. "OK, John," he said, "the stuff isn't on you. But there wasn't anybody else *out* here, just you, and you know your own rep—"

"The donkey," Dortmunder said.

Kelp blinked at him. "The what?"

"The guy in the donkey head. He walked around from the back to the front, and then he walked around again from the front to the back. We nodded at each other."

Kelp turned his hopeful hubcaps in his cousin's direction.

"The guy with the donkey head, that's who you—"

"What, Kelly?" demanded the cousin. "Kelly's my junior partner in this operation! He's been in it with me from the beginning, he's the director, he takes character roles, he *loves* this theater!" Glowering at Dortmunder, exuding more fertilizer essence than ever, cousin Bohker said, "So is *that* your idea, Mr. Dortmunder?" Dortmunder had been "John" before this. "Is *that* your idea? Cover up your own crime by smearing an innocent man?"

"Maybe *he* did it for a joke," Dortmunder said vengefully. "Or maybe he's absentminded."

Kelp, it was clear, was prepared to believe absolutely anything, just so they could all get past this social pothole. "Cuz," he said, "maybe so, maybe that's it. Kelly's your partner; maybe he took the money legit, spare you the trouble, put it in the bank himself."

But Bohker wouldn't buy it. "Kelly *never* touches the money," he insisted. "*I'm* the businessman, he's the ar-tiste, he's— Kelly!" he shouted through the entranceway, toward the stage, and vigorously waved his fat arm.

Kelp and Dortmunder exchanged a glance. Kelp's look was filled with a wild surmise; Dortmunder's belonged under a halo.

Kelly came out to join them, wiping his neck with a paper towel, saying, "What's up?" He was a short and skinny man who could have been any age from nine to 14 or from 53 to 80, but nothing in between. The donkey head was gone, but that didn't make for much of an improvement. His real face wasn't so much lined as pleated, with deep crevices you could hide a nickel in. His eyes were eggy, with blue yolks, and his thin hair was unnaturally black, like work boots. Except for the head, he was still in the same dumb costume, the idea having been that the actors in bib overalls and black T-shirts were supposed to be some kind of workmen, like plumbers or whatever, and the actors dressed in curtains and beach towels were aristocrats. Kelly had been the leader of the bunch of workmen who were going to put on the play within the play—oh, it was grim, it was grim—so here he was, still in his overalls and T-shirt. And black work boots, so that he looked the same on the top and the bottom. "What's up?" he said.

"I'll tell you what's up," Bohker promised him and pointed at Kelp. "I introduced you to my wife's cousin from the city."

"Yeah, you did already." Kelly, an impatient man probably wanting to get out of his work clothes and into something a little more actorly, nodded briskly at Kelp and said, "How's it goin'?"

"Not so good," Kelp said.

"And *this,*" Bohker went on, pointing without pleasure at Dortmunder, "is my wife's cousin's pal, also from the city, a fella with a reputation for being just a little light-fingered."

"Aw, well," Dortmunder said.

Kelly was still impatient: "And?"

"And he lifted the gate!"

This slice of jargon was just a bit too showbizzy for Kelly to grab on the fly like that; he looked around for a lifted gate, his facial pleats increasing so much he looked as though his nose might fall into one of the excavations. "He did *what?*"

Bohker, exasperated at having to use lay terminology, snapped, "He stole the money out of the box office."

"I did not," Dortmunder said.

Kelly looked at Dortmunder as though he'd never expected such treatment. "Gee, man," he said, "that's our eating money."

"I didn't take it," Dortmunder said. He was going for another run at dignity.

"He's got the gall, this fella," Bohker went on, braver about Dortmunder now that he had an ally with him, "to claim *you* took it!"

Kelly wrinkled up like a multicar collision: *"Me?"*

"All I said," Dortmunder told him, feeling his dignity begin to tatter, "was that you went around to the front of the theater."

"I did not," Kelly said. Being an actor, he had no trouble with dignity at all.

So he *did* do it, Dortmunder thought, and pressed what he thought of as his advantage: "Sure, you did. We nodded to each other. You were wearing your donkey head. It was about ten minutes before the show was over."

"Pal," Kelly said, "ten minutes before the show was over, I was on stage, asleep in front of everybody, including your buddy here. And without my donkey head."

"That's true, John," Kelp said. "The fairies took the donkey head away just around then."

"In that case," Dortmunder said, immediately grasping the situation, "it had to be one of the other guys in bib overalls. *They* weren't all on stage then, were they?"

But Bohker already had his mind made up. "That's right," he said. "That's what *you* saw, the big-town sharpie, when you came out of this box office right here, with the cash receipts in your pocket, and looked through that door right there in at that stage way back there, and saw Kelly was the only rustic on stage, and the donkey prop was gone, and—"

"The what?" Dortmunder had missed something there.

"The donkey prop!" Bohker cried, getting angrier, pointing at his own head. "The head! It's a prop!"

"Well, you know, Jesse," Kelly said thoughtfully, "in some union productions, you know, they'd call it a costume."

"Whatever it is," Bohker snapped, waving the gnats of show-biz cant away as though he hadn't summoned them up himself, then turning back to Dortmunder: "Whatever it is, you saw it, or *didn't* see it, when you looked right through there and saw Kelly asleep without his head, and none of the other rustics around, and right *then* you decided how you were gonna blame somebody else. And *I'm* here to tell you, it won't work!"

Well, innocence wasn't any help—overrated, as Dortmunder had long suspected—and dignity had proved to be a washout, so what was left? Dortmunder was considering violence, which usually tended at least to clear the air, when Kelp said, "Cuz, let me have a word in private with John, OK?"

"That's all I ever asked," Bohker said, with false reasonableness. "Just talk to your friend here, explain to him how we do things different in the country, how we don't take *advantage* of the kindness of people who take us *in* when we're on the *run,* how when we're away from the *city,* we behave like *decent, God-fearing*—"

"Right, cuz, right," Kelp said, taking Dortmunder by the elbow, drawing him away from the ongoing flow, nodding and nodding as though Bohker's claptrap made any sense at all, turning Dortmunder away, walking him back out toward the now nearly empty parking lot and across it to a big old tree standing there with leaves all over it, and Dortmunder promised himself, if Andy asks me even *once* did I do it, I'm gonna pop him.

Instead of which, once they'd reached the leafy privacy of the tree, Kelp turned and murmured, "John, we're in a bind here."

Dortmunder sighed, relieved and yet annoyed. "That's right."

"I dunno, the only thing I can think— How much did he say it was?"

"Two something. Something under three grand." And *that* got Dortmunder steamed in an entirely different way. "To think I'd stoop to grab such a measly amount of—"

"Sure you would, John, if the circumstances were different," Kelp said, cutting through the crap. "The question is, Can we cover it?"

"What do you mean, cover it?"

"Well, Jesse said if we give it back, he'll forget the whole thing, no questions asked."

Now Dortmunder was *really* outraged. "You mean, let the son of a bitch go on thinking I'm a thief?"

Kelp leaned closer, dropping his voice. "John, you *are* a thief."

"Not this time!"

"What does it matter, John? You're never gonna convince him, so forget it."

Dortmunder glared at the farmhouse, full now of actors, one of them with nearly three grand extra in his pocket. Probably looking out a window right now, grinning at him. "It's one of those guys," he said. "I can't let him get away with it."

"Why not? And what are you gonna do, play detective? John, we're not cops!"

"We watched cops work often enough."

"That isn't the same. John, how much money you got?"

"On me?" Dortmunder groused, reluctant even to discuss this idea, while out of the corner of his eye, he saw Kelly heading briskly toward the farmhouse. "Why *couldn't* it be him?" he demanded. "Partners steal from partners all the time."

"He was on stage, John. How much money you got?"

"On me, a couple hundred. In the suitcase, back at your god-damn cousin's house, maybe a grand."

"I could come up with eight, nine hundred," Kelp said. "Let's go see if we can cut a deal."

"I don't like this," Dortmunder said. "I don't go along with making restitution to begin with, and this is even worse."

Running out of patience, Kelp said, "What else are we gonna do, John?"

"Search that farmhouse there. Search the theater. You think some amateur can hide a stash so *we* can't find it?"

"They wouldn't let us search," Kelp pointed out. "We aren't cops, we don't have any authority, we can't throw any weight around. That's what cops do; they don't *detect,* you know that. They throw their weight around, and when you say, 'Oof,' you get five to ten in Green Haven. Come on, John, swallow your pride."

"I'm not gonna say I did it," Dortmunder insisted. "You wanna pay him off, we'll pay him off. But I'm not gonna say I did it."

"Fine. Let's go talk to the man."

They walked back to where cousin Bohker waited in the nar-row trapezoid of shade beside the barn. "Cuz," said Kelp, "we'd like to offer a deal."

"Admitting nothing," Dortmunder said.

"Two thousand, seven hundred twenty-four dollars," the cousin said. "That's the only deal I know."

"We can't quite come up with that much," Kelp said, "on ac-counta John here didn't actually take your money. But we know how things look and we know what John's reputation is—"

"Hey," Dortmunder said. "What about *you?*"

"OK, fine. The reputations we both have. So we feel we'll try to make good on what you lost as best we can, even though we didn't do it, and we could probably come up with two thousand. In and around two thousand."

"Two thousand, seven hundred twenty-four dollars," said the cousin, "or I call the troopers."

"Troopers?" Dortmunder stared at Kelp. "He's gonna call in the *Army*?"

"State troopers, he means." Kelp explained, and turned back to his cousin to say, "That wouldn't be a nice thing to do, cuz. Turn us over to the law and we're really in trouble. Can't you take the two—"

"Two thousand, seven hundred twenty-four dollars," said the cousin.

"Oh, the hell with this guy," Dortmunder abruptly said. "Why don't we just go take a hike?"

"I thought you might come up with that next," the cousin answered. He was smeared all over with smugness. "So that's why I sent Kelly for reinforcements."

Dortmunder turned, and there was Kelly back from the farmhouse, and with him were all the other rustics. Five of them, still in their bib overalls and T-shirts, standing there looking at Dortmunder and Kelp, getting a kick out of being the audience for a change.

It's one of them, Dortmunder thought. He's standing there and I'm standing here, and it's one of them. And I'm stuck.

Kelp said something, and then the cousin said something, and then Kelp said something else, and then Kelly said something; and Dortmunder tuned out. It's one of these five guys, he thought. One of these guys is a little scared to be out here, he doesn't know if he's gonna get away with it or not, he's looking at me and he doesn't know if he's in trouble or not.

Their eyes? No, they're all actors; the guy's gotta know enough to behave like everybody else. But it's one of them.

Well, not the fat one. You look at skinny Kelly there, and you see this fat one, and even with the donkey head on, you'd know it wasn't Kelly, having already seen Kelly in the first half, wearing the donkey head, and knowing what he looked like.

Hey, wait a minute. Same with the tall one. Kelly's maybe 5′5″ or 5′6″, and here's a drink of water must be 6′4″, and he stands all stooped, so if *he* had the donkey head on, the donkey's lips would be on his belt buckle. Not him.

Son of a gun. Two down. Three to go.

Conversation went on, quite animated at times, and Dortmunder continued to study the rustics. That one with the beard, well, the beard wouldn't show inside the donkey head, but look how hairy he is anyway; lots of bushy black hair on his head and very hairy arms below the T-shirt sleeves, all that black hair with the pale skin showing through. With the donkey head on, he'd look maybe a little *too* realistic. Would I have noticed? Would I have said, "Wow, up close, that's some hairy donkey?" Maybe, maybe.

Shoes? Black work boots, black shoes; some differences, but not enough, not so you'd notice.

Wait a minute. That guy, the one with the very graceful neck, the one who would be kept in the special block for his own protection if he were ever given five to ten at Green Haven, the one who moves like a ballet dancer; his bib overalls have a *crease*. Not him. He could cover himself in an entire donkey and I'd know.

Number five. Guy in his mid-20s, average height, average weight, nothing in particular about him except the watch. He's the guy, during the first half, while I'm waiting for it to be over, trying to find something to think about, he's the guy with the pale mark around his wrist where he usually wears a watch, so it isn't tanned. And now he's wearing the watch. Did the guy who walked by me have a pale mark on his wrist? Would I have noticed?

"John? John!"

Dortmunder looked around, startled out of his reverie. "Yeah? What is it?"

"What *is* it?" Kelp was looking frantic and he clearly wanted to know why Dortmunder wasn't frantic as well. "Do you think she could or not?" he demanded.

"I'm sorry," Dortmunder said, "I didn't hear the question. Who could what? Or not?" And thinking, it's either the hairy arms or the watch; hairy arms or watch.

"May," Kelp said, elaborately patient. "Do you think if you phoned May, she could send us a grand to pay off my cousin?"

Hairy arms or watch. Nothing shows on either face, nothing in the eyes.

"John? What's the *matter* with you?"

"Well," Dortmunder said, and put a big smile on his face, and even forced a little laugh, or something similar to a laugh, "well, you got us, cuz."

Kelp stared. *"What?"*

"Yeah, we took the money," Dortmunder said, shrugging. "But it was just for a joke, you know; we never meant to keep it."

"Yeah, I'm sure," Bohker said with a sarcastic smirk, while Kelp stood as though turned to stone. Limestone. In acid rain.

Kelly, cold and brisk, said, "Where is it?"

"Well, I don't know exactly," Dortmunder said. "I gave it to my partner to hide."

Kelp squawked; it sounded exactly like those chickens that a neighbor of Bohker's kept in his back yard. He squawked, and then he cried, "John! You never did!"

"Not you," Dortmunder told him. "My other partner, the actor in the cast here that's an old pal of mine. I slipped him the money and he went and hid it in the house." Hairy arms or watch; hairy arms or watch. Dortmunder turned and grinned easily at the kid with the pale band under his watch. "Didn't I?" he said.

The kid blinked. "I don't get you," he said.

"Aw, come on; the gag's over," Dortmunder told him. "If Bohker here calls his state troopers, I'll just tell them I gave you the money to hide and they'll go look in the house there and find it, and everybody *knows* I was never in that house, so it was you. So now the gag is over, right?"

The kid thought about it. Everybody standing there watched the kid thinking about it, and everybody knew what it meant that the kid had something to think about. The kid looked around and saw what it was that everybody knew, and then he laughed and clapped his hands together and said, "Well, we sure had them going there for a while, didn't we?"

"We sure did," Dortmunder said. "Why don't you and me go in the house now and get the cousin his money back?"

Bohker, sounding tough, said, "Why don't we *all* go in and get the goddamn money?"

"Now, now," Dortmunder said, mild as could be, "why don't you let us have our little secrets? We'll go in and we'll come out with the money. You'll get your money back, cousin, don't worry."

Dortmunder and the kid walked across the parking lot and up the stoop and across the porch full of gaping actors and went into the house. The kid led the way upstairs and down the hall and into the third room on the left, which contained two narrow beds and two small dressers and two wooden chairs. "Hold it a second," Dortmunder said, and looked around, and saw the one dresser drawer open about three inches. "Taped it to the back of the dresser drawer," he said.

"OK, OK, you're Sherlock Holmes," the kid said, sounding bitter. He went over and pulled the drawer out and put it on the bed. Masking tape held a bulky white envelope to the back of the drawer. The kid peeled it off and handed it to Dortmunder, who saw that it had a printed return address on the upper left corner: BOHKER & BOHKER, FERTILIZER & FEED.

"How'd you figure it out?" the kid asked.

"Your shoes," Dortmunder said. Which was a variant on the old untied-shoelace gag, because when the kid looked down at his shoes, what he saw was Dortmunder's fist coming up.

Outside again, Dortmunder crossed to the waiting rustics and held the envelope out in front of himself, flap open, so everybody could see the money wadded inside. "OK?"

Kelly said, "Where's Chuck?"

"Resting."

Bohker reached for the envelope, but Dortmunder said, "Not yet, cuz," and tucked the envelope inside his shirt.

Bohker glowered. "Not yet? What are you playing at, fella?"

"You're gonna drive Andy and me to your house," Dortmunder told him, "and we're gonna pack, and then you're gonna drive us to the bus depot, and when the bus comes in, I'll hand you this envelope. Play around, I'll make it disappear again."

"I'm not a vengeful fella," Bohker said. "All I care about is I get my money back."

"Well, that's one difference between us," Dortmunder said, which Bohker maybe didn't listen to hard enough.

Bohker's station wagon was one of the few cars left in the parking lot. Bohker got behind the wheel, his cousin Kelp beside him, and Dortmunder got in back with the old newspapers and cardboard cartons and fertilizer brochures and all the junk, and they drove off toward town. Along the way, Bohker looked in the rearview mirror and said, "I been thinking about what happened back there. You didn't take the money at all, did you?"

"Like I said."

"It *was* Chuck."

"That's right."

Kelp twisted around to look over the back of the seat and say, "John, how did you figure out it was him? That was goddamn genius."

If Kelp wanted to think what had happened was genius, it

would be better for Dortmunder to keep his thought processes to himself, so he said, "It just come to me."

Bohker said, "You had to mousetrap Chuck like you did or he'd have just denied it forever."

"Uh-huh."

"Well, I owe you an apology," Bohker said, being gruff and man to man about it.

"That's OK," Dortmunder told him.

"And there's no reason you fellas have to move out."

"Oh, I think we're ready to go, anyway," Dortmunder said. "Aren't we, Andy?"

"Yeah, I think so," Kelp said.

As Bohker turned the station wagon in to the driveway at his house, Dortmunder said, "Does that glove compartment lock?"

"Yeah, it does," Bohker said. "Why?"

"I tell you what we'll do," Dortmunder told him. "We'll lock this envelope in there for safekeeping, and you give me the key off the ring, and when we get on our bus, I'll give it back to you. On account of I know you don't trust me."

"Now, that's not fair," Bohker said defensively, parking beside his house. "I apologized, didn't I?"

"Still," Dortmunder said, "we'll both be happier if we do it this way. Which key is it?"

So Bohker took the little key off his key ring, and he and Kelp watched Dortmunder solemnly lock the envelope away in the crowded, messy glove compartment, and an hour and 45 minutes later, on the bus to Buffalo, Kelp turned in his seat and said, "You did, didn't you?"

"Sure, I did," Dortmunder agreed, taking wads of Bohker's money out of his pants pockets. "Treat me like that, threaten me with *troopers*."

"What's cousin Bohker looking at in that envelope?"

"Fertilizer brochures."

Kelp sighed, probably thinking about family complications.

"Still, John," he said, "you can hardly blame the guy for jumping to conclusions."

"I can if I want," Dortmunder said. "Besides, I figured I earned this, with what he put me through. That stuff, what's-it. Anguish, you know the kind. Mental, that's it. Mental anguish, that's what I got," Dortmunder said, and stuffed the money back into his pockets.

THE DORTMUNDER
WORKOUT

WHEN DORTMUNDER WALKED INTO THE O.J. BAR & GRILL ON
Amsterdam Avenue that afternoon, the regulars were talking
about health and exercise, pro and con. "A healthy regime is
very important," one of the regulars was saying, hunched over
his beer.

"You don't mean 'regime,'" a second regular told him. "A
healthy regime is like Australia. You mean 'regimen.'"

"'Regimen' is women," a third regular put in. "Something
about women."

The other regulars frowned at that, trying to figure out if it
meant anything. In the silence, Dortmunder said, "Rollo."

Rollo the bartender, observing the world from a three-point
stance—large feet solidly planted on the duckboards behind the
bar, elbow atop the cash register drawer—seemed too absorbed
either by the conversation or in contemplation of the possibility
of health to notice the arrival of a new customer. In any event,
he didn't even twitch, just stood there like a genre painting of
himself, while the first regular said, "Well, whatever the word is,
the point is, if you got your health you got everything."

"I don't see how that follows," the second regular said. "You
could have your health and still not have a Pontiac Trans Am."

"If you got your health," the first regular told him, "you don't need a Pontiac Trans Am. You can walk."

"Walk where?"

"Wherever it was you were gonna go."

"St. Louis," the second regular said, and knocked back some of his tequila sunrise in satisfaction.

"Well, now you're just being argumentative," the first regular complained.

"Some of that health stuff can get dangerous," the third regular put in. "I know a guy knew a guy had a heart attack from the Raquel Welch workout video."

"Well, sure," the first regular agreed, "it's always possible to exercise too *much,* but—"

"He wasn't exercising, he was just watching."

"Rollo," Dortmunder said.

"When I was in the Army," the first regular said, "they used to make us do sailor jumps."

"If you were in the Army," the second regular told him, "they were soldier jumps."

"Sailor jumps," insisted the first regular.

"We used to call those jumping jacks," the third regular chimed in.

"You did not," the second regular told him. "Jumping jacks is that little girl's game with the lug nuts."

"Rollo," Dortmunder demanded, and this time Rollo raised an eyebrow in Dortmunder's direction, but then he was distracted by movement from the third regular, the jumping jacks man, who, with a scornful "*Lug* nuts!" climbed off his stool, paused to wheeze and then said, "*This* is jumping jacks." And he stood there at a kind of crumpled attention, arms at his sides, heels together, chest in.

The second regular gazed upon him with growing disgust. "That's *what?*"

"It isn't sailor jumps, I know that much," the first regular said.

But the third regular was unfazed. "This is first position," he explained. "Now watch." Carefully, he lifted his right foot and moved it about 18 inches to the side, then put it back down on the floor. After stooping a bit to be sure he had both feet where he wanted them, he straightened up, more or less, faced forward, took a deep breath you could hear across the street and slowly lifted both arms straight up into the air, leaning his palms against each other above his head. "Position two," he said.

"That's some hell of an exercise," said the second regular.

The third regular's arms dropped to his sides like fish off a delivery truck. "When you're really into it," he pointed out, "you do it faster."

"That *might* be sailor jumps," the first regular admitted.

"In my personal opinion," the second regular said, twirling the dregs of his tequila sunrise, "diet is the most important part of your personal health program. Vitamins, minerals and food groups."

"I don't think you got that quite right," the third regular told him. "I think it goes, animal, vitamin or mineral."

"Food groups," the second regular contended. "This isn't twenty questions."

The first regular said, "I don't get what you mean by this food groups."

"Well," the second regular told him, "your principal food groups are meat, vegetables, dessert and beer."

"Oh," the first regular said. "In that case, then, I'm OK."

"Rollo," Dortmunder begged.

Sighing like an entire Marine boot camp, Rollo bestirred himself and came plodding down the duckboards. "How ya doin?" he said, flipping a coaster onto the bar.

"Keeping healthy," Dortmunder told him.

"That's good. The usual?"

"Carrot juice," Dortmunder said.

"You got it," Rollo told him, and reached for the bourbon bottle.

Party Animal

THERE WAS NO USE GOING ANY FARTHER DOWN THE FIRE ESCAPE. More cops were in the yard: A pair of flashlights white-lined the dark down there. From above, the *clonk-clonk* of sensible black shoes continued to descend on rusted metal stairs. A realist, Dortmunder stopped where he was on the landing and composed his soul for 10 to 25 as a guest of the state. American plan.

What a Christmas present.

A window, left of his left elbow. Through it, a dimly lighted bedroom, empty, with brighter light through the door ajar opposite. A pile of coats on the double bed. Faint party chatter wafting out through the top part of the window, open two inches.

An open window is not locked. It was a cold December out here. Dortmunder was bundled in a peacoat over his usual working uniform of black shoes, slacks and shirt—but with the party going on in there, the window had been opened at the top to let out excess heat.

Sliiide. Now open at the bottom. *Sliiide.* Now closed. Dortmunder started across the room toward that half-open door.

"Larry," said the pile of coats in a querulous female voice. "There's somebody in here."

The pile of coats could do a snotty male voice, too: "They're just going to the john. Pay no attention."

"And putting down my coat," Dortmunder said, dropping his

peacoat with its cargo of burglar tools and knickknacks from the corner jeweler, from where he had traveled up and over rooftops to this dubious haven.

"Ouch!" said the girl's voice.

"Sorry."

"Get on with it, all right?" Boy's voice.

"Sorry."

A herd of cops went slantwise downward past the window, their attention fixed on the darkness below, the muffled clatter of their passage hardly noticeable to anyone who didn't happen to be (a) a habitual criminal and (b) on the run. Despite the boy's advice to get on with it, Dortmunder stayed frozen until the last of the herd trotted by, then he took a quick scan of the room.

Over there, the shut door outlined in light would lead to the bathroom. The darker one would be . . . a closet?

Yes. Hurried, in near darkness, Dortmunder grabbed something or other from inside the closet, then shut that door again and moved quickly toward the outlined one as the girl's voice said, "Larry, I just don't feel comfortable anymore."

"Of course you don't."

Dortmunder entered the square, white bathroom—light-green towels, dolphins on the closed shower curtain—ignored the two voices departing from the room outside, one plaintive, the other overbearing, and studied his haberdashery selection.

Well. Fortunately, most things go with black, including this rather weary sports jacket of tweedy tan with brown leather elbow patches. Dortmunder slipped it on and it was maybe two sizes too big, but not noticeable if he kept it unbuttoned. He turned to the mirror over the sink, and now he might very well be a sociology professor—specializing in labor relations—at a small Midwestern university. A professor without tenure, though, and probably no chance of getting tenure, either, now that Marx has flunked his finals.

Dortmunder's immediate problem was that he couldn't hide. The cops knew he was in this building, so sooner or later some group of police officers would definitely be gazing upon him, and the only question was, how would they react when that moment came? His only hope was to mingle, if you could call that a hope.

Leaving the bathroom, he noticed that the pile of coats was visibly depleted. Seemed like everybody's plans were getting loused up tonight.

But this gave him a chance to stash his stash, at least temporarily. Finding his peacoat at last—already it was at the bottom of the pile—he took the jeweler's former merchandise and stowed it in the top left dresser drawer amid some other gewgaws and gimcracks. His tools went into the cluttered cabinet under the bathroom sink, and then he was ready to move on.

Beyond the partly opened bedroom door was a hall lined with national park posters. Immediately to the right, the hall ended at the apartment's front door. To the left, it went past a couple of open and closed doors till it emptied into the room where the party was. From here, he could see half a dozen people holding drinks and talking. Motown versions of Christmas songs bubbled along, weaving through the babble of talk.

He hesitated, indecisive, struck by some strange stage fright. The apartment door called to him with a siren song of escape, even though he knew the world beyond it was badly infested by law. On the other hand, a crowd is supposed to be the ideal medium into which a lone individual might disappear, and yet he found himself reluctant to test that theory. To party or not to party—that was the question.

Two events pushed him to a decision. First, the doorbell next to him suddenly clanged like a fire engine in hell, causing him to jump a foot. And second, two women emerged from the party into the hallway, both moving fast. The one in front looked to be in her early 20s, in black slacks and black blouse and white half-apron and red bow tie and harried expression; she carried an empty round silver tray and she veered off into the first door-way on the right. The second woman was older but very well put together, dressed in baubles and beads and dangling ear-rings and a whole lot of Technicolor makeup, and her expression was grim but brave as she marched down the hall toward Dort-munder.

No, toward the door. This was, no doubt, the hostess, on her way to answer the bell, wondering who'd arrived so late. Dort-munder, knowing who the late arrivals were and not wanting to be anywhere near that door when it opened, jackrabbited into motion with an expression on his face that was meant to be a party smile. "How's it goin'?" he asked with nicely understated amiability as they passed each other in the middle of the hall.

"Just *fine*," she swore, eyes sparkling and voice fluting, her own imitation party smile glued firmly in place. So she didn't know everybody at her party. Dortmunder could have been brought here by an invited guest, right? Right.

The party, as Dortmunder approached it, was loud, but not loud enough to cover the sudden growl of voices behind him. He made an abrupt turn into the open doorway that the harried woman had gone through and then he was in the kitchen, where the harried woman was putting a lot of cheese-filled tarts onto the round tray.

Dortmunder tried his line again: "How's it goin'?"

"Rotten," the harried woman said. Her ash-blonde hair was coiled in a bun in back, but much of it had escaped to lie in parabolas on her damp brow. She'd have been a good-looking woman if she weren't so bad-tempered and overworked. "Jerry never showed up," she snapped, as though it were Dort-munder's fault. "I have to do it all—" She shook her head and made a sharp chopping motion with her left hand. "I don't have time to talk."

"Maybe I could help," Dortmunder suggested. The growl of cop voices continued from back by the apartment door. They'd check the room next to the fire escape first, but then they'd be coming this way.

The woman looked at him as though he were trying to sell her magazine subscriptions: "Help? What do you mean, help?"

"I don't know anybody here." He was noticing: She was all in black, he was all in black. "I came with Larry, but now he's talking to some girl, so why don't I help out?"

"You don't help the caterer," she said.

"OK. Just a thought." No point getting her suspicious.

But as he was turning away, she said, "Wait a minute," and when he looked back, her sweat-beaded brow was divided in half by a vertical frown line. She said, "You really want to help?"

"Only if you could use some."

"Well," she said, reluctant to admit there might be something in this world for her not to be mad at, "if you really mean it."

"Count on it," Dortmunder told her. Shucking out of the borrowed jacket, looking around the room for a white apron like hers, he said, "It'll give me something to do other than just stand in the corner by myself. I'll take those things out, pass them around, you can get caught up."

Once the jacket was off and hanging on a kitchen chair, Dortmunder looked exactly like what he was: a semihardened criminal, a hunted man, a desperate fugitive from justice and a guy who just keeps slipping the mind of Lady Luck. This was not a good image. Failing to find a white apron, he grabbed a white dish towel instead and tucked it sideways across the front of his trousers. No red bow tie like the woman's, but that couldn't be helped.

She watched him suiting up. "Well, if you really want to do this," she said, and suddenly her manner changed, became much more official, commanding—even bossy. "What you have to do is remember to keep moving. It's a jungle out there."

"Oh, I know that," Dortmunder said.

"You don't want to get caught."

"Absolutely not."

"You'll get people," she said, making hand gestures to demonstrate the point, "who'll just keep grabbing and grabbing. You get into the middle of a conversational group, all of a sudden you can't get out without knocking somebody over, and then—that's a no-no, by the way," she interrupted herself.

Dortmunder had been nodding, one ear cocked for the approach of society's defenders, but now he looked quizzical and said, "A no-no?"

"Knocking over the guests."

"Why would I do that?" he asked. You knock over jewelry stores, not guests. Everybody knows that.

"If you're stuck in the middle of a group and there's no way out," she explained, "they'll eat everything on the tray. They're like a bunch of locusts, and there you are, and most of the other guests haven't had anything at all."

"I see what you mean. Keep moving."

"And," she said, "stick the tray into the middle, but don't go into the middle."

"I got it," he promised her. "I'm ready to make the move."

"You'll be fine."

"Sure," he said, and picked up the tarts and went to the aid of the party.

The party consisted of several clumps of people, mostly crowded around the bar, which was a serve-yourself table in front of curtained windows at one end of the long living room. Most people ignored the big cut-glass bowl of eggnog and went straight for the wine or the hard stuff. At the opposite end of the room stood the Christmas tree, short and fat and shedding, with many tiny colored lights that blinked on and off as if to say *chickee-the-cops, chickee-the-cops, chickee-the-cops.* I know, Dortmunder thought back at them, I know about it, all right?

A sofa and some chairs had been shoved against the walls to make room for the party, so everybody was standing, except one heavy woman dressed in a lot of bright fluttery scarves who perched on the sofa holding a glass as she talked to various people's stomachs. Occasionally, someone would bend down to say a friendly word to her forehead, but mostly she was ignored; the party was taking place at the five-foot level, not the three-foot level. And, as at most Christmas parties, everybody was looking a little tense thinking about all those lists at home.

Feeling the guard-dog eyes of the law scrape at his back, though the search party hadn't yet made its way down the hall, Dortmunder held the tray chest high and followed it into the scrum. People parted at the arrival of food, paused in drink and talk to take a tartlet, then closed ranks again in his wake. Sidling to the center of the crush, in the party but not of it, Dortmunder began to relax and to pick up shreds of conversation as he motored along:

"There's only twenty guys gonna be let in on this thing. We have seven already, and once we have all of the seed money. . . ."

"She came to the co-op board in a false beard and claimed she was a proctologist. Well, naturally. . . ."

"So then I said you can have this job, and he said OK, and I said you can't treat people like that, and he said OK, and I said that's it, I quit, and he said OK, and I said you're gonna have to get along without me from here on in, buster, and he said OK . . . so I guess I'm not over there anymore."

"And then these guys in a rowboat—no, wait, I forgot. First they blew up the bridge, see, and then they stole the rowboat."

"Merry Christmas, you Jew bastard, I haven't seen you since Ramadan."

"And he said, 'Madam, you're naked,' and I said, 'These happen to be *gloves,* if you don't mind,' and that shut him up."

"Whatever you want, Sheila. If you want to go, we'll go."

Wait a minute, that was a familiar voice. Dortmunder looked around, and another familiar voice, this one female, said, "I didn't say I wanted to leave, Larry. Why do you always put it on me?"

The couple from the coats. Dortmunder steered his tart tray in that direction, and there they were, both in their mid-20s, wedged into a self-absorbed bubble inside the larger party. Larry was very tall, with unnecessarily wavy dark hair and a long thin nose and long thin lips and little widely spaced eyes. Sheila was on the short side, a pretty girl, but with an extra layer of baby fat, driveway-colored hair and not much clothes sense; either that, or she'd just recently put on those extra pounds and hadn't bought any new clothes for the new body.

Dortmunder inserted the depleted tartlet tray into their space as Larry said, "I don't put it on you. You weren't happy in the other room, and now you're not happy here. Make your own decisions, that's all."

She turned her worried look to the tarts, but Larry grandly waved the tray away. Neither of them looked directly at Dortmunder. In fact, nobody looked directly at the server (*not* servant, please, in egalitarian America) where tartlets simply appeared in one's hand at a given point during the party.

Moving on through the throng, Dortmunder heard one last exchange behind him. ("Lately, you do this all the time." "*I'm* not doing anything, Sheila, it's up to you.") But his attention was diverted by an event ahead: The cops had arrived.

Three of them, uniformed, stocky, mustached, irritable. They were so grumpy that the Technicolor hostess in their midst looked as though she were under arrest.

But she wasn't under arrest, she was bird-dogging, eyeing the guests for the cops, looking for cuckoos in the nest. Unfamiliar faces, unfamiliar faces. . . .

Meanwhile, all the faces had grown just a little more rigid. It's hard to be aware that three bad-tempered cops are looking at you and pretend you aren't aware of it, and at the same time present an image that shows you're innocent of whatever it is they think you're guilty of, when you don't know what they think you're guilty of, and for all you know you are. Complex. No wonder every drink in the room was being drained more rapidly, even the club sodas and ginger ales.

Someone else was also observing the scene: the harried woman caterer. She'd been circulating in another part of the room with another tray, and she'd noticed the new arrivals. Dortmunder caught her looking from him to the cops and back again, and in the space between her damp hair and perky red bow tie, her thunderclouded face was an absolute emblem of suspicion. Doesn't anybody believe in altruism anymore?

Well, it was time to grasp the tiger by the tail and face the situation. The best defense is a good despair; Dortmunder marched directly to that dark blue cloud in the doorway, shoved his tray into its middle and said, "Tarts?"

"No, no," they said, brushing him away—even cops don't look at servers—and they went back to saying to the hostess, "Anybody you don't know. Anybody at all."

Dortmunder dallied nearby, offering his last few tarts to the closest convivials as he eavesdropped on the manhunt. The hostess was a rich contralto; under most circumstances, she would have been a pleasure to listen to, but these were not most circumstances: "I don't see anyone. Well, that person came with Tommy, his name is, oh, I'm so bad at names."

"It's faces we care about," one of the cops said, and damn near looked at Dortmunder.

Who realized it was time to move on. Unloading the last of his tarts, he segued into the empty kitchen, where he briefly

considered his circumstances, contemplated a cut-and-run and
decided this was no time to become a moving target.

On a cookie sheet on the kitchen counter lay a regiment of two-
inch-long celery segments, each filled with red-dyed anchovy
gunk. Green and red, Christmas colors; pretty, in a way, but not
particularly edible-looking. Nevertheless, he arranged these on
his tray, making a spiral, getting caught up in the design, attempting to make a Santa Claus face, failing, then picking up
the tray, and as he turned to leave, one of the cops walked in.

Dortmunder couldn't help himself; he just stood there. Deep
down inside, a terrific struggle was going on, invisible on the surface. You're a waiter, he told himself in desperation, you're with
the caterer, nothing else matters to you. Trying to build a per-
formance using the Method. But no. It didn't matter how he
spurred himself, he just went on standing there, tray in hands,
waiting to be led away.

The cop glared around the room as though he were pretty
sure somebody was there. His gaze slid off Dortmunder's furrowed brow, moved on, kept searching.

I *am* a waiter! Dortmunder thought, and almost smiled; except a waiter wouldn't. He took a step toward the door, and the
cop said, "Whose coat is that?"

Who's he talking to? There's nobody here but the waiter.

"You," the cop said, not quite looking in Dortmunder's direction. He pointed at the jacket Dortmunder had worn in here
from the bedroom. "That yours?"

"No." Which was not only the truth, it was also the simplest
possible answer. So rarely is the truth the simplest possible answer that Dortmunder, pleased by the coincidence, repeated it.
"No," he said again, then added a flourish for the hell of it. "It
was here when I came in."

The cop picked up the jacket and patted its pockets. Then he turned, draping the jacket over his arm, and Dortmunder, in the part at last, extended the tray. "You want a, a thing?"

The cop shook his head. He still wasn't looking at Dortmunder. He went away with the jacket, and Dortmunder sat on the now jacketless chair to have a quiet nervous breakdown. The hostess was going to say, "Why, that's my husband's jacket. In the kitchen? What was it doing there?" Then all the cops would come back and lay hands on him, and he would never be heard from again.

The harried woman steamed in, her own tray empty. Dortmunder got to his feet and said, "Just resting a minute."

She raised a meaningful brow in his direction.

Which he pretended not to see. "The cops didn't want the tarts," he said.

"I wonder what they did want," she said, still with that meaningful look.

"Maybe the party's too noisy," Dortmunder suggested. "Maybe the neighbor upstairs complained."

"That many cops? The neighbor upstairs must be the police commissioner."

"That's probably it," Dortmunder said. "What do you think? Should I make a special tray for them?"

"For the police?" This question brought her back to earth, and to business. "Nonguests are not our concern," she said. "What's that you're taking out there?" She peered at his tray much more suspiciously than she'd peered at him; good. "Ah, the anchovy logs," she said, nodding her approval.

"Anchovy logs?"

"You don't have to mention the name, just distribute them. And stick to the area at the other end of the room from the bar to move people away from the drinks."

"These logs," Dortmunder pointed out, "will drive them right back to the drinks."

"That's OK. Circulation's the name of the game."

The hostess came fluttering in, saying, "We have to *do* something. Can you *believe* this? Police!"

"We noticed," the harried woman said.

"Police ruin a party," the hostess announced.

"They sure do," Dortmunder agreed.

He should have kept his mouth shut; this just made the hostess focus on him, saying, "Jerry, what you should do is—" She blinked. "You're not Jerry."

"Sure I am," Dortmunder said, and flashed the tray of logs. "I better get out there," he said, scooting through the door. From behind he heard the harried woman say, "A different Jerry."

In the living room, the party wasn't really ruined at all. The cops were nowhere in sight and the partygoers were peacefully at graze once more. Dortmunder moved his tray hither and yon, away from the bar, and soon the hostess returned, but she was not at ease. She kept flashing worried looks toward the hall.

Hmmm. His tray still half full of logs, Dortmunder eased away from the party, skirted the hostess at some little distance and proceeded down the hall to reconnoiter, tray held out in front of himself as a *carte d'identité.*

He heard them before he saw them, a cop voice saying, "Which coat is yours?" Then he made the turn into the bedroom and there were the three cops, plus two more cops, plus two male partygoers, who looked worried and guilty as hell as they pawed through the pile of coats. "Snack?" Dortmunder inquired.

All the cops looked at him, but with annoyance, not suspicion. "Geddada here," one of them said.

"Right." Dortmunder bowed from the waist, like butlers in the old black-and-white movies on TV, and backed out of the room. Moving down the hall toward the party, he considered the possibility that one or both of those suspects would prove to have some sort of illegal substance in his coat. A happy thought, but would it sufficiently distract the law? Probably not.

Back at the party, Dortmunder unloaded more anchovy logs, and then somebody put two glasses onto his not-quite-empty tray and said, "Two white wines, pal."

Dortmunder looked at the glasses, then looked up, and it was his buddy Larry again, who turned away to continue pistol-whipping his girlfriend, saying, "Make your own decisions for yourself, Sheila, don't put the blame on me."

Bewildered, she said, "The blame for what?"

The waiter wasn't supposed to get drinks for people, was he? Everybody else was getting his own. Dortmunder considered tucking the two glasses inside Larry's shirt, but then he glanced over and saw a cop briefly in the doorway, looking around. He decided a waiter was somebody who waited on people, not somebody who knocked people around, so he carried the tray to the drinks table. The cop was gone again. Dortmunder filled one glass with white wine and the other with tonic and carried them back on the tray, being careful to give Sheila the wine. She was saying wistfully, "It just seems as though you're trying to push me away, but making it my fault."

So she was catching on, was she? Airily, Larry smirked at her and said, "It's all in your mind."

Dortmunder made a rapid retreat to the kitchen, not wanting to be in sight when Larry tasted the tonic, and now this room was absolutely full of cops talking to the harried woman, one of them saying, "You been here since the beginning of the party?"

"We're *catering* the party," she said. "We had to be here an hour before it started, to set up the food and the bar."

The cop gave Dortmunder a full frontal stare. "Both of you?"

"Of course both of us," the harried woman said. To Dortmunder she said, "Tell them, Jerry. We got here at six-thirty."

"That's right," Dortmunder told the cops, then turned to his partner in crime to say, "They're still hungry out there."

"We'll give them the shrimps now," she decided, and gestured for Dortmunder to join her at the counter next to the sink, where plastic pots of cold peeled shrimp and glass bowls of red sauce awaited.

The cops stood around and growled together while Dortmunder and the harried woman worked, their fingers sliding on the slippery shrimp. At last, though, the law left the room, and Dortmunder whispered, "Thanks."

"I don't know what you did—"

"Mistaken identity."

"All I know is, you saved my sanity. Also, I still need help with these shrimp."

"You got it."

"There's one thing, though, that I have to tell you," she said as they arranged shrimp on decorative plates. "I'm married."

"So am I," Dortmunder said. "Kinda."

"Me, too," she agreed. "Kinda. But for real."

"Sure," Dortmunder said. "We're just trays of shrimp that pass in the night."

"Right."

Returning to the party, Dortmunder saw Larry at the drinks table, a wrinkled look around his mouth as he poured a glass of white wine. Dortmunder kept out of his way as he circulated, distributing shrimp. The two suspects from the bedroom came back, looking shaken but relieved, and both beelined to the drinks table, where they made quite a dent.

A few minutes later, the apartment door thudded shut with a sound that gonged all the way down the hall and into the room with the party, where a whole lot of tense smiles suddenly loosened up.

Really? Gone? Given up? Dortmunder, suspicious by nature

and cautious by necessity, carried his half-full tray of shrimp and sauce down the empty hall, glanced into the empty bedroom, opened the apartment door and looked out at five cops looking in.

Umm. Two of them were women cops. All five were just standing around the corridor with faintly eager and hungry looks, like lions in the Colosseum. Behind them, the door to the apartment across the hall was propped half-open.

OK. So they still think the odds are that their missing burglar is at the party, so they've set up this corridor equivalent of a radar trap. Each partygoer on the way out will be taken into the apartment across the hall—with that good citizen's cooperation and approval, no doubt—and frisked. The women cops are for the women partygoers. And all five were looking at Dortmunder as though he were their first customer.

Uh-uh. True, he didn't have the stash on him, but the identity papers he carried were in case of routine stops, not for anything serious. These documents were like vampires, they crumbled when exposed to light.

Dortmunder extended the tray, "Have a shrimp?"

"We're on duty," one of the women cops said, and the other cops looked faintly embarrassed.

"Maybe later," Dortmunder suggested, and he closed the door on all those official eyes before they got the idea to dry-run their little gauntlet on the help.

What now? Eventually, this party, like all good things, must end. Until then, he was probably more or less safe, but as things stood, there was absolutely no way for him to get out of this apartment. Until they got their hands on the burglar, the police would not relax their vigilance for a second.

Until they got their hands on the burglar. Until they got their hands on *somebody*.

Play the hand. Dortmunder slipped sideways into the bedroom, balancing the tray one-handed as he opened the dresser

drawer where he'd stashed the stash. He was careful about his selection; a proper Christmas gift should be something you'd like
to receive yourself, so he resisted the impulse to keep the best
swag for himself, instead choosing to sacrifice two brooches and
a bracelet that were definitely cream of the crop. These went into
his pants pocket and back out of the bedroom he eased, on the
alert.

And here came Larry and Sheila down the hall away from the
party, he still assuring her that she was the one making all the decisions, while she wore the expression of someone who can't figure
out what it is that keeps biting her on the ass. They would all
meet at the midpoint of the hall, with just enough room for everybody to get by.

Well, it could have been anybody, but, in fact, Dortmunder
had been thinking about Larry a bit, anyway. The guy was a
smart-aleck, which was good; he'd be more likely to think he
could bullshit the cops the way he was doing Sheila, more likely
to rub them the wrong way and attract their attention. And
now this business of sidestepping past one another in the hall
just made it easier.

"I don't want to go if *you* don't want to go," Sheila was saying, her eyes phosphorescent with tears that hadn't yet started
to fall, and at that point in the middle of Larry's long-suffering
sigh, darned if the server didn't almost dump his whole tray of
shrimp and red sauce all over Larry's shirt. "Hey! Watch it!"

"Oops! Here, let me—"

"That's all right, that's all right, no harm done, everything's
fine, if you don't mind," Larry said with an aggressive, splay-
fingered brushing down of his front, where nothing had actually
spilled but where the server had been apologetically pawing and
patting.

Timing is all. Dortmunder made his way back to the party, dis-
tributed the rest of his shrimp among the needy, and when he

saw the harried woman, empty-trayed, heading for the kitchen, he followed her.

Now she was putting little sausages on the tray, each with its own yellow toothpick. Dortmunder reached into his pocket for the one prize he hadn't given Larry: an extremely nice gold brooch shaped like a feather. "Hold it," he said, walking over behind her, and tucked it into the raveled bun of her hair.

"What? What? What's that?" She didn't know what was happening but was afraid to turn her head.

"When you get home," Dortmunder advised, "have your guy fish that out of there. Not before."

"But what is it?"

"A feather," he said accurately, and disrobed himself of the dish towel he'd been hiding behind. Too bad that jacket wasn't around anymore. "Well," he said, "up the chimney I speed."

She laughed, a happier person than when they'd met, and picked up her refilled tray. "Say hello to the elves."

"I will."

They both left the kitchen, she to continue her good works and he moving briskly but without unseemly haste down the hall toward the apartment door, through which, as he neared it, came the muffled sound of voices raised in dispute, among them the high tones of the perhaps unnecessarily loyal Sheila.

"Just who do you think you are?" And that was Larry, bless him.

Eventually, of course, Larry's innocence—at least in this context—would be established, and the manhunt would resume. But by then the wily perpetrator would be long gone. Flexing into the bedroom, the wily perpetrator found his peacoat at the bottom of the pile again and refilled it quickly and silently with his tools and the evening's profits. Before leaving, he paused briefly to pick up the bedside phone and dial his faithful companion, May, waiting for him at home, who answered by saying "Wrong number," which was her form of

preemptive strike against possible breathers and objection-
able conversationalists.

"I'm a little bit late, May," Dortmunder said.

"You certainly are," May agreed. "Where are you, the precinct?"

"Well, I'm at a party," Dortmunder said, "but I'll be leaving
in a minute." Leaving, to be specific, to continue his interrupted
descent of the fire escape. "There was a complication," he explained, "but it's OK now."

"Is it a nice party?"

"The food's good," Dortmunder said. "See you soon."

GIVE TILL IT HURTS

IT WAS HARD TO RUN, DORTMUNDER WAS DISCOVERING, WITH your pockets full of bronze Roman coins. The long skirt flapping around his ankles didn't help, either. This hotel is either too damn big, he told himself, huffing and puffing and trying to keep his pants up under this bulky white dress, or it's too small.

Okay, the dress isn't really a dress, it's an aba, but it gets in the way of running legs just as much as any dress in the world. How did Lawrence of Arabia do it, in that movie that time? Probably trick photography.

Also, the sheet on his head, called a keffiyeh, held on by this outsize cigar band circlet called an akal, is fine and dandy if you're just walking around looking at things, but when you run it keeps sliding over your eyes, particularly when you have to go around a corner and not run straight into the wall, like now.

Dortmunder turned the corner, and here came a half dozen of his fellow conventioneers, Arabian numismatists jabbering away at each other and kicking their skirts out ahead of them as they walked. How did they *do* that?

Dortmunder braked hard to a walk, to a stroll, and fixed a brotherly smile on his face as he approached the approaching sheiks, or whatever they were. "Sawami," he said, using the one word he'd found that seemed to work. "Sawami, sawami."

They all smiled back, and nodded, and said some stuff, and proceeded on around the corner. With any luck, the cops would arrest one of *them*.

Here's the thing. If you happen to hear that in a big hotel in midtown Manhattan there's going to be a sale of ancient coins, where most of the dealers and most of the customers are going to be rich Arabs, what can you possibly do but dress yourself up like a rich Arab, go to the hotel, mingle a little, and see what falls into your pockets? If the dealer with the heavy beard and the loud voice hadn't also happened to see what was falling into Dortmunder's pocket, everything would have been okay. As it was, he'd eluded pursuit so far, but if he were to try to leave the hotel by any of its known exits he was pretty sure he'd suddenly feel a lot of unfriendly hands clutching at his elbows.

What to do, what to do? Getting out of this OPEC drag wouldn't help much, since his pursuers had no doubt already figured out he was a goof in sheik's clothing. In fact, wearing it helped him blend in with the hotel's regular guests, so long as he didn't have to engage in conversation more complicated than, "Sawami sawami. Sawami? Ho, ho, sawami!"

And at least he wasn't up in Santa Claus rig. Every year around this time, with shiny toys in the store windows and wet snow inside your shoes, wherever there might happen to be any kind of a robbery in a public setting, the cops *immediately* would nick the nearest Saint Nick, because it is well known that Santa Claus is every second-rate second story guy's idea of a really terrific disguise.

Not Dortmunder. Better a sheet among sheiks than a red suit, a white pillow and handcuffs. Leave your camel at home.

NO ADMISSION. That was what the door said, and that was perfect. That was exactly what you would look for when you're on the run, a door that says *No Admission*, or *Authorized Personnel Only*, or *Keep Out:* any of those synonyms for 'quick-exit.' This particular door was at a turn in the corridor, tucked away mostly out of sight in the corner of the L. Dortmunder looked down both lengths of empty hallways, tried the knob, found it locked, and stepped back to consider just what kind of lock he was expected to go through here.

Oh, that kind. No problem. Hiking up his skirt, reaching into a coin-laden pants pocket, he brought out a little leather bag of narrow metal implements he'd once told an arresting officer was his manicure set. That cop had looked at Dortmunder's fingernails and laughed.

Dortmunder manicured *No Admission,* pushed the door open, listened, heard no alarm, saw only darkness within, and stepped through, shutting the door behind him. Feeling around for a lightswitch, his fingers bumped into some sort of shelf, then found the switch, flipped it up, and a linen closet sprang into existence: sheets, towels, tissue boxes, soap, quart-size white plastic coffee pitchers, tiny vials of shampoo. Well, hell, *this* was no way out.

Dortmunder turned and reached for the doorknob and felt a breeze. Yes? He turned back, inspecting the small but deep crowded room with all his eyes, and there at the rear was a window, an ordinary double hung window, and its bottom half was just slightly open.

What floor am I on? Dortmunder had gone out windows before in his career that had turned out to be maybe a little too high up in the air for comfort and he'd lived to regret it, but at least he'd lived. But where was he now?

The window was behind shelves piled with towels. Dortmunder moved towels out of the way, leaned his head in between two shelves, pushed the window farther open and looked out into December darkness. A kind of jumbled darkness lay in an indefinite number of stories below, maybe three, maybe five. To the right were the backs of tall buildings facing 57th Street and to the left were the backs of shorter buildings facing 56th Street.

Didn't people make rope ladders out of sheets? They did; Dortmunder followed their example, first tying the end of a sheet around the handle of a coffee pitcher and lowering that out the window, then tying sheets together and paying them out until he heard the far-away *clunk* of the pitcher against something hard.

Far away.

Don't look down, Dortmunder reminded himself, as he tied the top sheet to a shelf bracket and stripped at last out of his Middle East finery and switched off the linen closet light, but then he had to figure out how to get this body from this position, standing in the dark linen closet, to hanging on sheets outside the window. How do you get from here to there? To slide between the shelves and out the window head first seemed utter folly; you'd wind up pointing the wrong way, and you wouldn't last long. But to get up on the shelf and through that narrow opening feet first was obviously impossible.

Well, the impossible takes a little longer, particularly in the dark. *Many* parts of himself he hit against the wooden edges of the shelves. Many times he seemed certain to fall backward off a shelf and beat his head against the floor. Many times he had all of himself in position except one arm, on the wrong shelf, or maybe one knee, that had found a way to get into the small of his back. Then there came a moment when all of him was outside the window except his left leg, which wanted to stay. Ultimately, he was reduced to holding onto the sheet with his teeth and right knee while pulling that extra leg out with both hands, then in a panic grabbing the sheet with every molecule in his body just as he started to fall.

The sheets held. His hands, elbows, knees, thighs, feet, teeth, nostrils and ears held. Down he went, the cold city breeze fanning his brow, his descent accompanied by the music of ancient coins clinking in his pocket and tiny threads ripping in the sheets.

The jumbled darkness down below was full of *stuff,* some of it to be climbed over, some to be avoided, none of it friendly. Dortmunder blundered around down there for a while, aware of that white arrow on the side of the hotel in the evening dark, pointing its long finger directly at him, and then he saw, up a metal flight of stairs, a metal grillwork door closed over an open doorway, with warm light from within.

Maybe? Maybe. Dortmunder tiptoed up the stairs, peered through the grill, and saw a long high room completely encased by books. A library of some kind, well lit and totally empty, with a tall Christmas tree halfway along the left side.

Dortmunder manicured the metal door, stepped through, and paused again. At this end of the room were a large desk and chair, at the far end a long marble-topped table, and in between various furniture; sofa, chairs, round table. The Christmas tree gave off much bright light and a faint aroma of the north woods. But mostly the room was books, floor to the ceiling, glowing amber in the warmth of large faceted overhead light globes.

At the far end was a dark wooden door, ajar. Dortmunder made for this, and was halfway there when a short gray-haired guy came in, carrying two decks of cards and a bottle of beer. "Oh, hi," the guy said. "I didn't see you come in. You're early."

"I am?"

"Not *very* early," the guy conceded. Putting the cards on the round table and the beer on a side table, he said, "I have this right, don't I? You're the fella Don sent, to take his place, because he's stuck at some Christmas party."

"Right," Dortmunder said.

"Pity he couldn't make it," the guy said. "He always leaves us a few bucks." He stuck his hand out. "I'm Otto, I didn't quite get your . . ."

"John," Dortmunder said, fulfilling his truth quota for the day. "Uh, Diddums."

"Diddums?"

"It's Welsh."

"Oh."

Two more guys came into the room, shucking out of topcoats, and Otto said, "Here's Larry and Justin." He told them, "This is John Diddums, he's the guy Don sent."

"Diddums?" Justin said.

"It's Welsh," Otto explained.

"Oh."

Larry grinned at Dortmunder and said, "I hope you're as bad a player as Don."

"Ha ha," Dortmunder said.

Okay; it looks like there's nothing to do but play poker with these people, and hope the real substitute for Don doesn't show up. Anyway, it's probably safer in here, for the moment. So Dortmunder stood around, being friendly, accepting Otto's offer of a beer, and pretty soon Laurel and Hardy came in, Laurel being a skinny guy called Al and Hardy being a nonskinny guy called Henry, and then they sat down to play.

They used chips, a dollar per, and each of them bought twenty bucks worth to begin. Dortmunder, reaching in his heavy pockets, pulled out with some wadded greenbacks a couple of bronze coins, which bounced on the floor and were picked up by Henry before Dortmunder could get to them. Henry glanced at the coins and said, as he put them on the table and pushed them toward Dortmunder, "We don't take those."

Everybody had a quick look at the coins before Dortmunder could scoop them up and slip them back into his pocket. "I've been traveling," he explained.

"I guess you have," Henry said, and the game began. Dealer's choice, stud or draw, no high-low, no wild cards.

As Dortmunder well knew, the way to handle a game of chance is to remove the element of chance. A card palmed here, a little dealing of seconds there, an ace crimped for future reference, and pretty soon Dortmunder was doing very well indeed. He wasn't winning every hand, nothing that blatant, but by the time the first hour was done and the cops began to yell at the metal grillwork door Dortmunder was about two hundred forty bucks ahead.

This was Otto's place. "Now what?" he said, when all the shouting started out back, and got to his feet, and walked back there to discuss the situation through the locked grill.

Looking as though he didn't believe it, or at least didn't want to believe it, Al said, "They're raiding our poker game?"

"I don't think so," said Henry.

Otto unlocked the door, damn his eyes, and the room filled up with a bunch of overheated uniformed cops, several of them with new scars and scrapes from running around in that jumbled darkness out there. "They say," Otto told the table generally, "there was a burglary at the hotel, and they think the guy came this way."

"He scored some rare coins," one cop, a big guy with sergeant's stripes and Perry on his nameplate, said. "Anybody come through here tonight?"

"Just us," Larry said. Nobody looked at Dortmunder.

"Maybe," one of the cops said, "you should all show ID."

Everybody but Dortmunder reached for wallets, as Otto said, "Officer, we've known each other for years. I own this building and the bookshop out front, and these are writers and an editor and an agent, and this is our regular poker game."

"You all know each other, huh?"

"For years," Otto said, and grabbed a handy book, and showed the cop the picture on the back. "See, that's Larry," he said, and pointed at the guy himself, who sat up straight and beamed a big smile, as though his picture was being taken.

"Oh, yeah?" The cop looked from the book to Larry and back to the book. "I read some of your stuff," he said. "I'm Officer Nekola."

Larry beamed even more broadly. "Is that right?"

"You ever read William J. Caunitz?" the cop asked.

Larry's smile wilted slightly. "He's a friend of mine," he said.

"Of ours," Justin said.

"Now there's a real writer," Nekola said. "He used to be a cop himself, you know."

"We know," Larry said.

While the literary discussion went on, Dortmunder naturally found himself wondering: Why are they covering for me here? I came in the back way, I showed those coins, they don't know me for years, so why don't they all point fingers and shout, "Here's your man, take him away!" What's up? Isn't this carrying the Christmas spirit a little too far?

The symposium had finished. One of the cops had gotten Justin to autograph a paperback book. The cops were all leaving, some through the front toward the bookstore, the rest returning to the jumbled darkness out back. Otto called after them, "In case anything comes up, how do we get in touch with you people?"

"Don't worry," Sgt. Perry said. "We'll be around for hours yet."

And then Dortmunder got it. If these people were to blow the whistle, the cops would immediately take him away, meaning he would no longer be in the game. *And he had their money.*

You don't do that. You don't let a new guy leave a poker game after one measly hour, not if he has your money, not for *any* excuse. And particularly under these current circumstances. Knowing what they now knew about Dortmunder, his new friends here would be replaying certain recent hands in their minds and seeing them in a rather different light.

Which meant he knew, unfortunately, what was expected of him now. If this is the quid, that must be the quo.

Otto resumed his seat, looking a bit grim, and said, "Whose deal?"

"Mine," Justin said. "Draw, guts to open."

Dortmunder picked up his cards, and they were the three, five and seven of spades, the queen of hearts and the ace of clubs. He opened for the two dollar limit, was raised, and raised back. Everybody was in the hand.

Since it didn't matter what he did, Dortmunder threw away the queen and the ace. Justin dealt him two replacements and he looked at them, and they were the four and six of spades.

Has anybody ever done that before? Dortmunder had just drawn twice to an inside straight in the same hand, and made it. And made a straight flush as well. Lucky, huh? If only he could tell somebody about it.

"Your bet, John," Justin said.

"I busted," Dortmunder said. "Merry Christmas." He tossed in the hand.

It was going to be a long night. Two hundred and forty dollars long.

JUMBLE SALE

Dortmunder having come into possession of some certain coins of a particular value, and the merchant named Stoon having recently returned to the slammer upstate, he decided it was time to go see Arnie Albright. Nothing else to be done. Therefore, shrugging his shoulders and pocketing his Ziploc bag of coins, Dortmunder took the West Side IRT up to 86th, then walked on up to 89th between Broadway and West End, where Arnie's apartment moldered upstairs over a bookstore.

Dortmunder entered the vestibule. He thought about ringing the doorbell there, but then he thought about not ringing it, and liked that thought better, so he went through the interior door with a shrug of a credit card. Climbing the stairs, he stopped at Arnie's door—it was a particularly offensive shade of dirty gray-yellow-green—and rapped the metal with his knuckles.

Nothing.

Was Arnie out? Impossible. Arnie was never out. It was practically against a city ordinance for Arnie Albright to go out of his apartment and mingle with ordinary people on the ordinary street. So Dortmunder rapped again, with the knuckle of the middle finger of his right hand, and when that still produced nothing he kicked the door instead, twice: KHORK, KHORK.

"WHAT?" demanded a voice from just the other side of the door.

Dortmunder leaned close. "It's me," he said, not too loudly. "John Dortmunder."

"DORTMUNDER?"

"Who you tryin' to tell, the people in Argentina?"

Many lock noises later, the door opened and Arnie Albright stood there, the same as ever, unfortunately. "Dortmunder," Arnie cried, already exasperated. "Whyn'tchoo ring the doorbell, like a person?"

"Because then you yell at me on the intercom," Dortmunder explained, "and you want me to yell back, and tell my business to everybody on the street."

"I gotta protect myself," Arnie said. "I got things of value here." He gestured vaguely behind himself, as though he couldn't quite remember which things of value they were, or where exactly he'd put them.

Dortmunder said, "You gonna let me in?"

"You're here, aren't you?" Arnie, a grizzled, gnarly guy with a tree-root nose, a skinny, deeply lined person who could have been any age from four hundred to a thousand, stepped back and gestured Dortmunder inside, saying, "So Stoon's been sent up again, huh?"

Surprised, because this was very new news, Dortmunder said, "When'd you hear that?"

Arnie shut the door. "I didn't. But when I see you coming to Arnie, I know Stoon's outta business."

"Oh, naw," Dortmunder said.

"Don't tell me, Dortmunder," Arnie said, leading the way across the living room, if that's the word. "If Stoon was out and about, up and around, coming and going, it's him you'd go see in a minute, even though I pay better dollar."

"Naw, Arnie," Dortmunder said, following, wishing he didn't have to spend so much time lying when he was with Arnie.

The Albright apartment had small rooms with big windows, all of them looking out past a black metal fire escape at a panoramic view of the brick rear wall of a parking garage maybe four feet away. For interior decoration, Arnie had hung a lot of his calendar collection around on the walls, all of these Januaries starting on all different days of the week, with numbers in black or red or, very occasionally, dark blue. Also, to break the monotony, there were the calendars that started in March or August, the ones Arnie called incompletes. (Being a serious collector, he was full of serious collector jargon.) The top halves of all these calendars were pictures, mostly photographs (fall foliage, kittens in baskets, the Eiffel Tower), except that the pictures of the girls bent way over to pump gas into a roadster were drawings. Excellent drawings in very bright colors, really artistic. Also, the religious pictures, mainly the Sermon on the Mount (perspective!), were drawings, but generally not as artistically interesting as the girls.

Arnie led the way through the decades to the table over by the parking garage view, saying, "So what have you got for me today? Huh? Not a piano, I bet, huh? Not a piano? Huh?"

It was amazing how quickly Arnie could become tiresome. "Some coins, Arnie," Dortmunder said.

"Damn, you see?" Arnie said. "It didn't work."

"It didn't?"

"Just the other day," Arnie said, his voice full of accusation, "I read this self-improvement thing, see, in some goddam magazine in the garbage, 'Lighten Up, Asshole,' something like that, it said, 'Laugh and the world laughs with you, piss and moan and you piss and moan alone.'"

"I heard that," Dortmunder allowed. "Something like that."

"Well, it's bullshit," Arnie said. "I just tried a joke there—"

"You did?" Dortmunder looked polite. "I'm sorry I missed it."

"It's my personality that's wrong," Arnie said. "It's just who I am, that's all. Somebody else could tell that joke, you'd be on the floor, you'd need CPR, the Heimlich Maneuver. But not me. I'm a pain in the ass, Dortmunder, and don't argue with me about that."

"I never argue with you, Arnie," Dortmunder said.

"I get on people's nerves," Arnie insisted. He waggled a bony finger in Dortmunder's face. "I make them sorry they ever met me," he snarled. "It don't matter what I do, I even put on perfume, would you believe it?"

"Well," Dortmunder said cautiously, "you *do* smell kinda different at that, Arnie."

"Different, yeah," Arnie growled. "Not better, just different. I put on these *male scents,* you know what I mean? Ripped 'em outta some other magazine, outta the trash can up at the corner, rubbed 'em all over myself, now people get close to me, they hail a *cab* to get away."

Dortmunder sniffed, not a lot. "It's not that bad, Arnie," he said, though it was.

"At least you lie to me," Arnie said. "Most people, I'm so detestable, they can't *wait* to tell me what a turd I am. Well, sid-down by the window there, that'll help a little."

Dortmunder sat by the open window, at the wooden chair by the table there, and it did help a little; the honest reek of old parking garage and soot helped to cut the cloying aromas of Arnie, who smelled mostly like a giant package of artificial sweetener gone bad.

On this old library table Arnie had long ago laid out a number of his less valuable incompletes, attaching them with a thick layer of clear plastic laminate. Dortmunder now took out his Ziploc bag and emptied it in the middle of the table, onto a June where two barefoot, freckle-faced, straw-hatted lads were just arriving at the old fishin' hole. "This is what I got," he said.

Arnie's dirty, stubby fingers brushed coins this way and that. "You been travelin', Dortmunder?" he wanted to know. "Seein' the world?"

"Is that one of those jokes, Arnie?"

"I'm just askin'."

"Arnie," Dortmunder said, "the Roman Empire isn't there anymore, you can't visit, it's been gone, I dunno, a hundred years, maybe. More."

"Well, let's see," Arnie said, giving nothing away. From his rumpled clothing he withdrew a piece of old rye bread and a jeweler's loupe. Putting the bread back where he'd found it, he tucked the loupe into his left eye and bent to study the coins, one at a time.

"They're good," Dortmunder assured him. "It's a big sale of the stuff, at a hotel in midtown."

"Mm," Arnie said. He lifted one coin, and bit it with his back teeth.

"It isn't an oreo, Arnie," Dortmunder said.

"Mm," Arnie said, and the doorbell rang.

Arnie lifted his head. For one horrible moment, the loupe stared straight at Dortmunder, like somebody looking out a door's peephole without the door. Then Arnie put his left hand in front of himself on the table, palm up, lifted his left eyebrow, and the loupe fell into his palm. "There," he said, "*that's* what you should do, Dortmunder. Ring the doorbell."

"I'm already here."

"Lemme just see what this is."

Never knowing when it might become necessary to remove oneself to a different location, Dortmunder scooped the ancient coins back into the Ziploc bag, and the bag back into his pocket, as Arnie crossed to the intercom grid near the door, pressed the button, and said, "WHAT?"

"*That's* why I don't," Dortmunder muttered.

A voice, distorted by all the kinks in the intercom wires, *bracked* from the grid: "*Arnie Albright?*"

"WHO WANTS TO KNOW?"

"*Petey Fontana.*"

"NEVER HEARDA YA."

"*Joe sent me.*"

Arnie turned to cock a look at Dortmunder, who pushed his

chair back a bit from the table. The fire escape was a very comforting presence, just outside this open window.

"WHICH JOE? JERSEY JOE OR PHILLY JOE?"

"*Altoona Joe.*"

Arnie reared back, releasing the button. He showed Dortmunder a gaze rich in wonder and confusion. "There really is an Altoona Joe," he whispered.

"Never heard of him," Dortmunder said.

"He's inside, been in awhile. Petey Fontana?"

"Never heard of him either."

The doorbell rang. Arnie whirled back, stabbing the button: "HOLD ON!"

"*We're just standin' around out here.*"

"WHO'S WE'RE?"

"*My partner and me.*"

Arnie released the button and frowned at Dortmunder in an agony of indecision. "Now a partner," he said.

"Let them in or not," Dortmunder suggested.

"Why didn't *I* thinka that?" Arnie turned to chop at the button: "WHADAYA HEAR FROM JOE?"

"He's still in Allentown, another two three clicks."

Button release; turn to Dortmunder. "And that's true, too. I'm gonna let them in, Dortmunder. Don't say a word."

Dortmunder nodded, not saying a word.

"You're my cousin from outta town."

"No," Dortmunder said. "I'm from the block association, I'm here to talk to you about a contribution."

Arnie glowered. "Now you don't even wanna be related to me."

"It isn't that, Arnie," Dortmunder lied. "It's, we don't look that much alike."

"Neither did Cain and Abel," Arnie said and turned back to push the button once more: "COME ON UP." He pushed the other button, and the buzz sound could be heard, faintly, from far away downstairs.

Dortmunder stood and pulled his chair around with its back to the wall, so it wasn't exactly at the table anymore, but the fire escape was still extremely handy. Then he sat down again. Arnie opened the apartment door and stood there looking out and down the stairs. Feet could be heard. A normal human voice, without intercom distortion, said, "Arnie Albright?"

"I didn't change in one flight a stairs," Arnie said. "Come in."

Two people came in, and it wasn't hard at all to tell which one was Petey Fontana. He was the non-woman. He was maybe 30, a little bulky, black-haired, blue-jawed, in chinos and thick shoes and a maroon vinyl jacket with a zipper. The woman was very similar to Petey, except her short hair was yellow, her jaw was white, and her vinyl jacket was robin's-egg blue.

It wasn't a total surprise that Petey Fontana's partner should be a woman. Crime has been a politically correct gender-blind equal-opportunity career for a long long time, much longer than fireperson or mailperson or even doctorperson. Bonnie Parker, Ma Barker, Leona Helmsley; the list goes on.

Petey and the woman stopped in the middle of the room and looked at Dortmunder, who got to his feet and smiled like he was just a stranger here, passing through. Arnie shut the door and came around his new guests to say, "So Altoona Joe sent you, huh?"

"Yeah," Petey Fonanta said. He was still looking at Dortmunder.

"Altoona Joe can't stand my guts," Arnie remarked, and shrugged. "But neither can anybody else. And the same with you two."

The woman said, "What? What's the same with us two?"

"By the time you leave here," Arnie told her, "you'll be so disgusted, all you'll want to do is punch Altoona Joe in the mouth, and there he is in the pen, safe. I'm surprised he didn't warn you about me, paint you one a them word pictures? You owe him money or something?"

Petey Fontana ignored all that, because he was still looking at Dortmunder, and now he said, out of the side of his mouth, "You didn't introduce your friend."

"Acquaintance," Dortmunder said.

Arnie said, "That's John—"

"Diddums," Dortmunder said, in a hurry, not knowing what Arnie might have come out with.

Petey Fontana frowned. The woman said, "Diddums?"

"It's Welsh."

"Oh."

Arnie said, "John's my cousin from outta town."

"Once removed," Dortmunder said, giving Arnie a dirty look.

Petey gestured at the woman: "This is my partner, Kate Murray. That's all she is, we're partners."

"That's right," Kate Murray said. She looked and sounded determined. "Just partners, that's it."

"And Altoona Joe sent you," Arnie said, looking thoughtful.

"He said, we come to town," Petey answered, "we should look you up."

"That's some friend you got there," Arnie said. "He sends you to *me,* just to chat."

"Well, we got something you might want," Petey said.

"Yeah," Kate said.

"And what would that be?" Arnie asked.

Petey lowered his eyebrows in Dortmunder's direction. "Can we talk in front of the cousin?"

"Why not?" Arnie asked. "He's still my cousin, no matter how much he removes."

Dortmunder said, "Blood is thicker than water."

Petey considered that. "They both spill the same," he said.

Kate said, "Petey, if it's gonna go down, let's do it."

Petey shrugged. "Okay." Turning at last away from Dortmunder and toward Arnie, he said, "What we got, we got television sets."

Arnie did an elaborate act of looking all over Petey, up and down, his clothing and hair and everything, before he said, "They must be awful *small* television sets, huh? Huh? Small sets? Huh?"

That was the joke again, going by there. Dortmunder recognized it this time, but he still didn't feel like laughing. And Petey just stood there and moved his shoulders like a guy overdo for a workout and said, "What?"

Arnie spread his hands at Dortmunder. "You see what I mean," he said. Then, to Petey, he said, "Where are these television sets?"

"In the truck outside."

Kate said, "You can have the truck, too."

"For trucks I got no interest," Arnie told her. "With the alternate side parking on this block, I wouldn't even have a tricycle. You found a parking place, huh?"

"We're double-parked out front," Petey said. "Which is why we'd like to move this transaction a little."

"Transaction," Arnie said, tasting the word. "So you got a truck out there with some televisions."

Kate said, "We got a extra-long semi with Ohio plates and four hundred television sets."

Arnie stared at her. "Double-parked on 89th Street?"

Kate said, "Where else would you put it?"

"It's not a question comes up a lot," Arnie said.

Petey, sounding impatient, said, "Well? Are you up for this or not?"

"You come all this way," Arnie told him, unruffled, "and you're such a good friend of Altoona Joe, the least I can do is look at the goods. Okay?"

"Sure." Petey nodded heavily at Arnie, and then nodded heavily at Kate, saying, "Stay with the cousin."

"Sure."

Petey and Arnie left, and Dortmunder said to Kate, "Why not sit down?"

"All right," she said, and sat on a lumpy brown sofa under a lot of January mountain ranges and waterfalls. Dortmunder took again his chair by the window, and she looked at him and said, "You here for a transaction, too?"

Transaction. Dortmunder said, "I'm here being a cousin, that's all. Once removed."

"You aren't in the business?"

Dortmunder looked very interested. "What business?" he asked.

"Never mind."

Conversation ceased after that, like a plant that's never been watered, until Arnie and Petey returned, arguing about the potential value of four hundred Taiwanese television sets in a depressed economy. "I gotta make a phone call," Arnie announced, "see can I get these things off my hands again, should it happen I put them *on* my hands in the first place. That is, if I can find somebody'll talk to a piece of crap like me, is what."

Arnie went into the other room, from where the faint murmur of his phone call could soon be heard. Petey sat on the sofa next to Kate and patted her knee, saying, "How's it going?"

"Fine."

Petey looked at Dortmunder. He smiled, which Dortmunder didn't believe at all, and said, "We interrupt you guys doin' business?"

"No, just being cousins," Dortmunder assured him.

"He's a civilian," Kate said.

Petey considered that, looking from Dortmunder to Kate and back. He seemed unconvinced, but didn't say anything, and conversation again dropped into nothingness.

Arnie walked into the room and looked around at the three silent people seated there. "What is this?" he wanted to know. "Did I die? Is this my wake? I didn't expect so many people."

Petey never much liked anything that anybody ever said about anything. Glowering at Arnie, he said, "So? Do we have a deal or not?"

"We have a wait," Arnie told him. "I hate to have to tell you this, but you're gonna have to put up with my presence a little while longer. Until the guy calls me back."

Kate, with a worried frown at her partner, said to Arnie, "How long?"

"Five minutes? Maybe ten minutes?"

Petey lifted his wrist to look at a watch the size of a pizza covered with black olives, and said, "Ten minutes. Then we're outta here."

Arnie said, "You want my cousin to drive the truck around while we wait?"

Petey gave him a look. "Do we look like we're worried about a ticket?"

Kate said, "And nobody's gonna *tow* a truck that size."

"You're right, there," Arnie said.

Funny how conversation kept dying. This group just didn't have much to say to one another. Also, Petey was not a patient kind of person, in the normal way of things, which was becoming increasingly evident. About the fourth time he looked at the pizza on his wrist, Arnie said, "I could turn on the radio, you like, find some music, you two could dance."

Petey glowered. "We're just partners," he said.

"Right, right, I forgot."

Dortmunder got to his feet, as though casual. "Well, cuz," he said to Arnie, "maybe I'll go back outta town."

Petey switched his glower to Dortmunder. "Why don't you stick around instead?" he said.

"Yeah, Door—Diddums," Arnie said. "Stick around."

Although Dortmunder did say, "I don't see why—" nobody heard him because at that moment a whole *lot* of pounding rattled the metal apartment door, and voices shouted, "Open up! Police! Police!"

Petey and Kate stared at one another wide-eyed. Dortmunder

stared at the fire escape; if Arnie could only stall the cops for thirty or forty seconds . . .

Arnie strode briskly to the apartment door and flung it open. "Took you guys long enough," he said.

Dortmunder and Petey and Kate all reacted to that remark, staring open-mouthed at Arnie as the room filled up with uniforms. There then followed a great deal of noise and confusion, during which Dortmunder and Petey and Kate found themselves standing in a row against a wall of Januaries—baseball players, old cars, chrome-covered diners—while a number of fierce-looking cops pinned them there with gimlet glares.

When at last there was comparative silence, except for everybody's heavy breathing, a plainclothesman came in through the open door and pointed his lumpy forehead at Arnie to say, "Arnie, what the hell are you up to?"

"Nothing, Lieutenant," Arnie said, "as you well know. I'm retired, and reformed, and off the fence."

"Crap," the lieutenant said, and sniffed. "What stinks in here?"

"Me," Arnie said. "As usual."

"Worse than usual, Arnie." The lieutenant's forehead considered Dortmunder and Petey and Kate. "What's with this unlovely crowd?"

"What I told you on the phone," Arnie reminded him. "Them two tried to sell me stolen TV sets."

Petey said, "We never said they were stolen."

"Sharrap," the lieutenant told Petey. To Arnie, he said, "These three, huh?"

"No, no, *them* two. That one's my cousin, John Diddums, from outta town."

"*First* cousin!" Dortmunder cried. In that moment, he became the only person in history ever to love Arnie Albright.

The lieutenant's forehead expressed all sorts of disbelief. "This isn't a crook?"

"Absolutely not," Arnie said. "I'm the black sheep of the

family, Lieutenant. John there, he's my inspiration for honesty. He runs the family grocery store in Shickshinny, Pennsylvania."

The lieutenant frowned at Dortmunder. "Where the hell is Shickshinny?"

"Pennsylvania," Dortmunder said, being in no mood to contradict Arnie.

The lieutenant thought things over. He said, "Arnie? You'll come downtown, make a statement?"

"Naturally," Arnie said. "I told you, I'm the straight goods now."

"Will wonders never cease." To his armed forces, the lieutenant said, "Take those two, leave that one."

Kate cried out, "This is a *hell* of a thing! Lou, what we—"

"Shut up, Kate," Petey said, and Kate shut up. But she fumed, as she and Petey were taken away by all the uniforms, followed by the lieutenant, who closed the door.

Dortmunder dropped into the chair by the window like something that had fallen out of an airplane. Arnie came over to sit across the table and say, "Quick, lemme see those coins. We don't got a whole lotta time."

Wondering, handing over the Ziploc bag, Dortmunder said, "Arnie? Why'd you turn those two in?"

"You kidding?" Loupe in eye, Arnie studied coins. "They were cops. Undercover. Entrapment, like they like to do. That's probably what got your pal Stoon."

"Cops? Are you sure?"

The loupe looked at Dortmunder; still an uncomfortable event. "What's the first thing they said when they come in? 'We're just partners.' Dortmunder? Were they just partners?"

"He put his hand on her knee, while you were out on the phone."

"They do the four-hand aerobics, am I right?"

"Sure. So?"

"If two regular, honest crooks walk in here," Arnie said, "and they're a guy and a broad, what do they care what we think about whether they're schtuppin' or not, am I right?"

"You're right."

"But an undercover cop," Arnie said, studying coins again, "when he's out on the job, he'll pretend to be a druggie, a burglar, a murderer, a spy, any goddam thing. He'll say he's anything at all, because everybody that matters knows he really isn't. But the one thing he can't say is he's getting it on with his partner, because when *that* gets home to the wife, she'll *know it's true.*"

"You had me very worried, Arnie," Dortmunder said. "I probably didn't show it, but I was very worried."

"They won't uncover themselves until they get downtown," Arnie said, "so we got a little time. Not much."

"Really very worried," Dortmunder said.

"I may be ugly, stupid, bad-smelling, antisocial, friendless and a creep," Arnie said, "but I don't get entrapped by officer Petey and officer Kate. I tell you what I'll do with these coins."

"Yeah?"

From his pocket Arnie took the piece of rye bread and a set of truck keys. The keys he dropped on a January of a boy carrying his girlfriend's books home from school down a country lane, and the bread he started to eat. "I palmed those when we went down to look at the goods," he said, around the stale bread. "I got no use for trucks *or* TVs, Dortmunder, but there's a guy over in Jersey—"

"I know him."

"An even swap," Arnie said. "I'll take the coins, you take the truck and the TVs."

"Done."

Dortmunder scooped in the keys and got to his feet. "Better give me the Ziploc bag, Arnie," he said.

"For why?"

"To carry the loot in."

Arnie gaped at him, bread an unlovely mass in his mouth. "The TVs and the truck? In a Ziploc bag?"

Dortmunder smiled upon him. "*That's* how you tell that joke, Arnie," he said, and got out of there.

NOW WHAT?

Everybody on the subway was reading the *Daily News,* and every newspaper was open to exactly the same page, the one with the three pictures. The picture of the movie star, smiling. The picture of the famous model, posing and smiling. And the picture of the stolen brooch. Shaped vaguely like a boomerang, with a large, dark stone at each end and smaller, lighter stones scattered between like stars in the night sky seen, say, from a cell, even the brooch seemed to be smiling.

Dortmunder was not smiling. He hadn't realized how big a deal this damn brooch would be. With pictures of the brooch in the hands of every man, woman and child in the greater New York metropolitan area, it was beginning to seem somehow less than brilliant that he should smuggle the thing into Brooklyn, disguised as a ham sandwich.

Over breakfast (sweetened orange juice, coffee with a lot of sugar, Wheaties with a *lot* of sugar), that concept had appeared to make a kind of sense, even to have a certain elegance. John Dortmunder, professional thief, with his sloped shoulders, shapeless clothing, lifeless hair-colored hair, pessimistic nose and rustyhinge gait, knew he could, if he wished, look exactly like your normal, average working man, even though, so far as he knew, he had never earned an honest dollar in his life. If called upon to transport a valuable stolen brooch from his home in Manhattan to a new but highly recommended fence in Brooklyn, therefore, it had seemed to him that the best way to do it was to place the brooch between two slabs of ham with a *lot* of mayonnaise, this package to be inserted within two slices of Wonder Bread, the result wrapped in paper towels and the whole carried inside an ordinary wrinkled brown paper lunch bag. It had *seemed* like a good idea.

Only now he didn't know. What was it about this brooch? Why was its recent change of possessor all over the *Daily News?*

The train trundled and roared and rattled through the black tunnel beneath the city, stopping here and there at bright-lit white-tile places that could have been communal showers in state prisons but were actually where passengers embarked and detrained, and eventually one such departing passenger left his *Daily News* behind him on the seat. Dortmunder beat a bag lady to it, crossed one leg over the other and, ignoring the bag lady's bloodshot glare, settled down to find out what the fuss was all about.

300G BROOCH IN DARING HEIST
Lone Cat Burglar Foils Cops, Top Security

Well, that wasn't so bad. Dortmunder couldn't remember ever having been called daring before, nor had anyone before this ever categorized his shambling jog and wheezing exertions as that of a cat burglar.

Anyway, on to the story:

"In town to promote his new hit film, *Mark Time III: High Mark,* Jer Crumbie last night had a close encounter with a rapid-response burglar who left the superstar breathless, reluctantly admiring and out the $300,000 brooch he had just presented his fiancée, Desiree Makeup spokesmodel Felicia Tarrant.

"'It was like something in the movies,' Crumbie told cops. 'This guy got through some really tight security, grabbed what he wanted and was out of there before anybody knew what happened.'

"The occasion was a private bash for the Hollywood-based superstar in his luxury suite on the 14th floor of Fifth Avenue's posh Port Dutch Hotel, frequent host to Hollywood celebrities. A private security service screened the invited guests, both at lobby level and again outside the suite itself, and yet the burglar, described as lithe, in dark clothing, with black gloves and a black ski mask, somehow infiltrated the suite and actually managed to wrest the $300,000 trinket out of Felicia Tarrant's hands just moments after Jer Crumbie had presented it to her to the applause of his assembled guests.

"'It all happened so fast,' Ms. Tarrant told police, 'and he was so slick and professional about it, that I still can't say exactly how it happened.'"

What Dortmunder liked about celebrity events was that they tended to snag everybody's attention. Having seen, both on television and in the *New York Post,* that this movie star was going to be introducing his latest fiancée to 250 of his closest personal friends, including the press, at his suite at the Port Dutch Hotel, Dortmunder had understood at once that the thing to do during the party was to pay a visit to the Port Dutch and drop in on every suite except the one containing the happy couple.

The Port Dutch was a midtown hotel for millionaires of all kinds—oil sheiks, arbitrageurs, rock legends, British royals—and its suites, two per floor facing Central Park across Fifth Avenue, almost always repaid a drop-in visit during the dinner hour.

Dortmunder had decided he would work only on the floors below the 14th, where the happy couple held sway, so as not to pass their windows and perhaps attract unwelcome attention. But on floor after floor, in suite after suite, as he crept up the dark fire escape in his dark clothing, far above the honking, milling, noisy red-and-white stage set of the avenue far below, he met only disappointment. His hard-learned skills at bypass-ing Port Dutch locks and alarms—early lessons had sometimes included crashing, galumphing flights up and down fire es-capes—had no chance to come into play.

Some of the suites clearly contained no paying tenants. Some contained occupants who obviously meant to occupy the suite all evening. (A number of these occupants' stay-at-home activi-ties might have been of educational interest to Dortmunder, had he been less determined to make a profit from the evening.)

A third category of suites was occupied by pretenders. These were people who had gone out for an evening on the town, leav-ing behind luggage, clothing, shopping bags, all visible from the fire escape windows, providing clues that their owners were second-honeymooners from Akron, Ohio who would repay an enterprising burglar's attentions with little more than Donald Duck sweatshirts from 42nd Street.

Twelve floors without a hit. The not-quite-honeymoon suite was just ahead. Dortmunder was not interested in engaging the attention of beefy men in brown private security guard uniforms, but he was also feeling a bit frustrated. Twelve floors, and not a sou: no bracelets, no anklets, no necklaces; no Rolexes, ThinkPads, smuggled currency; no fur, no silk, no plastic (as in credit cards).

OK. He would *pass* the party, silent and invisible. He would segue from 12 up past 14 without a pause, and then he would see what 15 and above had to offer. The hotel had 23 floors; all hope was not gone.

Up he went. Tiptoe, tiptoe; silent, silent. Over his right shoul-der, had he cared to look, spread the dark glitter of Central Park. Straight down, 140 feet beneath his black-sneakered feet, snaked the slow-moving southbound traffic of Fifth Avenue, and just up ahead lurked suite 1501-2-3-4-5.

The window was open.

Oh, now what? Faint party sounds wafted out like laughing gas. Dortmunder hesitated but knew he had to push on.

Inch by inch he went up the open-design metal steps, cool in the cool April evening. The open window, when he reached it, revealed an illuminated room with a bland pale ceiling but apparently no occupants; the party noises came from farther away.

Dortmunder had reached the fire escape landing. On all fours, he started past the dangerous window when he heard suddenly approaching voices:

"You're just trying to humiliate me." Female, young, twangy, whining.

"All I'm *trying* is to teach you English." Male, gruff, cocky, impatient.

Female: "It's a pin. Anybody knows it's a pin!"

Male: "It is, as I said, a brooch."

Female: "A brooch is one of them things you get at the hotel in Paris. For breakfast."

Male: "That, Felicia, sweetheart—and I love your tits—I promise you, is a *brioche*."

Female: "Brooch!"

Male: "*Bri-oche!*"

Most of this argument was taking place just the other side of the open window. Dortmunder, thinking it unwise to move, remained hunkered, half-turned so his head was just below the sill while his body was compressed into a shape like a pickup's spring right after 12 pieces of Sheetrock have been loaded aboard.

"You can't humiliate me!"

An arm appeared within that window space above Dortmunder's head. The arm was slender, bare, graceful. It was doing an overarm throw, not very well; if truth be told, it was throwing like a girl.

This arm was attempting to throw the object out through the open window, and in a way it accomplished its purpose. The flung object first hit the bottom of the open window, but then it de-flected down and out and wound up outside the window.

In Dortmunder's lap. Jewelry, glittering. What looked like emeralds on the ends, what looked like diamonds along the middle.

Any second now somebody was going to look out that win-dow to see where this bauble had gone. Dortmunder closed his left hand around it and moved. It was an automatic reaction, and since he'd already been moving upward he kept on moving upward, rounding the turn of the landing, heaving up the next flight of the fire escape, breathing like a city bus, while behind him the shouting began:

Male: "Hey! Hey! Hey! Hey! Hey!"

Female: "Oh, *no! Oh,* no! *Oh, no!*"

Up and over the hotel roof and into the apartment building next door and down the freight elevator and out onto the side street, a route long known to Dortmunder. When he at last am-bled around the corner onto Fifth, merely another late-shift worker going home, the police cars were just arriving in front of the hotel.

Newspapers tell lies, Dortmunder thought. He read on, to find a description of the thing in his ham sandwich. The things that looked like emeralds were emeralds, and the things that looked like diamonds were diamonds, that was why the fuss. Altogether, the trinket the bride-perhaps-to-be had flung ricocheting out the window last night was valued, in the newspapers, at least, at $300,000.

On the other hand, newspapers lie. So it would be up to Har-mov Krandelloc, said to be an ethnic so different from anybody else that no one had yet figured out even what continent he came from, but who had recently set himself up in a warehouse off Atlantic Avenue where it crossed Flatbush as king of the next generation of really worthwhile fences, who paid great dollar (sometimes even more than the usual ten percent of value) and never asked too many questions. It would be up to Harmov Krandelloc to determine what the thing in the ham sandwich was actually worth, and what Dortmunder could hope to realize from it.

But now, on the BMT into deepest Brooklyn, surrounded by newspaper photos of his swag, realizing that the celebrity of its former owners made this particular green-and-white object more valuable but also more *newsworthy* (a word the sensible burglar does his best to avoid), Dortmunder hunched with increasing despondency under his borrowed paper, clutched his brown bag in his left hand with increasing trepidation and wished fervently he'd waited a week before trying to unload this bauble.

More than a week. Maybe six years would have been right.

Roizak Street would be Dortmunder's stop. While keeping one eye on his *News* and one eye on his lunch, Dortmunder also kept an eye on the subway map, following the train's creeping progress from one foreign neighborhood to another; street names without resonance or meaning, separated by the black tunnels.

Vedloukam Boulevard; the train slowed and stopped. Roizak Street was next. The doors opened and closed. The train started, roaring into the tunnel. Two minutes went by, and the train slowed. Dortmunder rose, peered out the car windows and saw only black. Where was the station?

The train braked steeply, forcing Dortmunder to sit again. Metal wheels could be heard screaming along the metal rails. With one final lurch, the train stopped.

No station. Now what? Some holdup, when all he wanted to do—

The lights went out. Pitch-black darkness. A voice called, "I smell smoke." The voice was oddly calm.

The next 27 voices were anything but calm. Dortmunder, too, smelled smoke, and he felt people surging this way and that, bumping into him, bumping into one another, crying out. He scrunched close on his seat. He'd given up the *News,* but he held on grimly to his ham sandwich.

"ATTENTION, PLEASE."

It was an announcement, over the public address system.

Some people kept shouting. Other people shouted for the first people to stop shouting so they could hear the announcement. Nobody heard the announcement.

The car became still, but too late. The announcement was over. "What did he say?" a voice asked.

"I thought it was a she," another voice said.

"It was definitely a he," a third voice put in.

"I see lights coming," said a fourth voice.

"Where? Who? What?" cried a lot of voices.

"Along the track. Flashlights."

"Which side? What way?"

"Left."

"Right."

"Behind us."

"That's not flashlights, that's *fire!*"

"What! What! What!"

"Not behind us, buddy, in front of us! Flashlights."

"Where?"

"They're gone now."

"What time is it?"

"*Time!* Who gives a damn what time it is?"

"I do, knucklehead."

"Who's a knucklehead? Where are you, wise guy?"

"Hey! *I* didn't do anything!"

Dortmunder hunkered down. If the car didn't burn up first, there was going to be a first-class barroom brawl in here pretty soon.

Someone sat on Dortmunder. "Oof," he said.

It was a woman. Squirming around, she yelled, "Get your hands off me!"

"Madam," Dortmunder said, "you're sitting on my lunch."

"Don't you talk dirty to *me!*" the woman yelled, and gave him an elbow in the eye. But at least she got off his lap—and lunch—and went away into the heaving throng.

The car was rocking back and forth now; could it possibly tip over?

"The fire's getting closer!"

"Here come the flashlights again!"

Even Dortmunder could see them this time, outside the window, flashlights shining blurrily through a thick fog, like the fog in a Sherlock Holmes movie. Then someone carrying a flashlight opened one of the car's doors, and the fog came into the car, but it wasn't fog, it was thick oily smoke. It burned Dortmunder's eyes, made him cough and covered his skin with really bad sunblock.

People clambered up into the car. In the flashlight beams bouncing around, Dortmunder saw all the coughing, wheezing, panicky passengers and saw that the people with the flashlights were uniformed cops.

Oh, good. Cops.

The cops yelled for everybody to shut up, and after a while everybody shut up, and one of the cops said, "We're gonna walk you through the train to the front car. We got steps off the train there, and then we're gonna walk to the station. It's only a couple blocks, and the thing to remember is, stay away from the third rail."

A voice called, "Which is the third rail?"

"All of them," the cop told him. "Just stay away from rails. OK, let's go before the fire gets here. Not *that* way, whaddya looking for, a barbecue? *That* way."

They all trooped through the dark smoky train, coughing and stumbling, bumping into one another, snarling, using their elbows, giving New Yorkers' reputations no boost whatsoever, and eventually they reached the front car, where more cops—*more* cops—were helping everybody down a temporary metal stair-case to the ground. Of course it would be metal, with all these third rails around; it couldn't be wood.

A cop took hold of Dortmunder's elbow, which made Dort-munder instinctively put his wrists together for the cuffs, but the cop just wanted to help him down the stairs and didn't no-tice the inappropriate gesture. "Stay off the third rail," the cop said, releasing his elbow.

"Good thought," Dortmunder said, and trudged on after the other passengers, down the long smoky dark tunnel, lit by bare bulbs spaced along the side walls.

The smoke lessened as they went on, and then the platform at Roizak Street appeared, and yet another cop put his hand on Dortmunder's elbow, to help him up the concrete steps to the platform. This time Dortmunder reacted like an innocent per-son, or as close to one as he could get.

A lot of people were hanging around on the platform; appar-ently, they wanted another subway ride. Dortmunder walked through them, and just before he got to the turnstile to get out of here yet another cop pointed at the bag in his hand said, "What's that?"

Dortmunder looked at the bag. It was much more wrinkled than before and was blotchily gray and black from the sooty smoke. "My lunch," he said.

"You don't want to eat that," the cop told him, and pointed at a nearby trash can. "Throw it away, why don't ya?"

"It'll be OK," Dortmunder told him. "It's smoked ham." And he got out of there before the cop could ask for a taste.

Out on the sidewalk at last, Dortmunder took deep breaths of Brooklyn air that had never smelled quite so sweet before, then headed off toward Harmov Krandelloc, following the di-rections he'd been given: two blocks this way, one block that way, turn right at the corner, and there's the 11 paddy wagons and the million cops and the cop cars with all their flashing lights and the long line of handcuffed guys being marched into the wagons.

Dortmunder stopped. No cop happened to be looking in this direction. He turned smoothly around, not even disturbing the air, and walked casually around the corner, then crossed the street to the bodega and said to the guy guarding the fruit and vegetable display outside, "What's happening over there?"

"Let me get you a paper towel," the guy said, and he went away and came back with two paper towels, one wet and one dry.

Dortmunder thanked him and wiped his face with the wet paper towel, and it came away black. Then he wiped his face with the dry paper towel and it came away gray. He gave the paper towels back and said, "What's happening over there?"

"One of those sting operations," the guy said, "like you see in the movies. You know, the cops set up a fake fence operation, get videotape of all these guys bringing in their stuff, invite them all to a party, then they arrest everybody."

"When did they show up?"

"About ten minutes ago."

I'd have been here, Dortmunder thought, if it wasn't for the subway fire. "Thinka that," he said.

The guy pointed at his bag: "Whatcha got there?"

"My lunch. It's OK, it's smoked ham."

"That bag, man, you don't want that bag. Here, gimme, let me—"

He reached for the bag, and Dortmunder pulled back. Why all this interest in a simple lunch bag? What ever happened to the anonymous-workman-with-lunch-bag theory? "It's fine," Dortmunder said.

"No, man, it's greasy," the bodega guy told him. "It's gonna soak through, spoil the sandwich. Believe me, I know this shit. Here, lemme give you a new bag."

A paddy wagon tore past, behind Dortmunder's clenched shoulder blades, siren screaming. So did a second one. Meantime, the bodega guy reached under his fruit display and came out with a fresh new sandwich-size brown paper bag. "There's plastic people," he explained, "and there's paper people, and I can see you're a paper man."

"Right," Dortmunder said.

"So here you go," the guy said, and held the bag wide open for Dortmunder to transfer his lunch.

All he could hope was that no brooch made any sudden leap for freedom along the way. He opened the original bag, which in truth was a real mess by now, about to fall apart and very greasy and dirty, and he took the paper towel–wrapped sandwich out of it and put it in the fresh, crisp, sharp new paper bag, and the bodega guy gave it a quick twirl of the top to seal it and handed it over, saying, "You want a nice mango with that? Papaya? Tangelo?"

"No, thanks," Dortmunder said. "I would, but I break out."

"So many people tell me that," the bodega guy said, and shook his head at the intractability of fate. "Well," he said, cheering up, "have a nice day."

A paddy wagon went by, screaming. "I'll try to," Dortmunder promised, and walked away.

No more subways. One burning subway a day was all he felt up to, even if it did keep him from being gathered up in that sting operation and sent away to spend the rest of his life behind bars in some facility upstate where the food is almost as bad as your fellowman.

Dortmunder walked three blocks before he saw a cab; hang the expense, he hailed it: "You go to Manhattan?"

"Always been my dream," said the cabbie, who was maybe some sort of Arab, but not the kind with the turban. Or were they not Arabs? Anyway, this guy wasn't one of them.

"West 78th Street," Dortmunder said, and settled back to enjoy a smoke-free, fire-free, cop-free existence.

"Only thing," the Arab said, if he was an Arab. "No eating in the cab."

"I'm not eating," Dortmunder said.

"I'm only saying," the driver said, "on account of the sandwich."

"I won't eat it," Dortmunder promised him.

"Thank you."

They started, driving farther and farther from the neighborhood with all the paddy wagons, which was good, and Dortmunder said, "Cabbies eat in the cabs all the time."

"Not in the backseat," the driver said.

"Well, no."

"All's the space we can mess up is up here," the driver pointed out. "You eat back there, you spill a pickle, mustard, jelly, maybe a chocolate chip cookie, what happens my next customer's a lady in a nice mink coat?"

"I won't eat the sandwich," Dortmunder said, and there was no more conversation.

Dortmunder spent the time trying to figure out what the guy was, if he wasn't Arab. Russian, maybe, or Israeli, or possibly Pakistani. The name by the guy's picture on the dash was Mouli Mabik, and who knew what that was supposed to be? You couldn't even tell which was the first name.

Their route took them over the Brooklyn Bridge, which at the Manhattan end drops right next to City Hall and all the court buildings it would be better not to have to go into. The cab came down the curving ramp onto the city street and stopped at the traffic light among all the official buildings, and all at once there was a pair of plainclothes detectives right *there,* on the left, next to the cab, waving their shields in one hand and their guns in the other, both of them yelling, "You! Pull over! Right now!"

Oh, *damn* it, Dortmunder thought in sudden panic and terror, they *got* me!

The cab was jolting forward. It was not pulling over to the side, it was not obeying the plainclothesmen, it was not delivering Dortmunder into their clutches. The driver, hunched very low over his steering wheel, glared straight ahead out of his windshield and accelerated like a jet plane. Dortmunder stared; he's helping me escape!

Zoom, they angled to the right around two delivery trucks and a parked hearse, climbed the sidewalk, tore down it as the pedestrians leaped every which way to get clear, skirted a fire hydrant, caromed off a sightseeing bus, tore on down the street, made a screaming two-wheeled left into a street that happened to be one-way coming in this direction, and damn near managed to get between the oncoming garbage truck and the parked armored car. Close, but no cigar.

Dortmunder bounced into the bulletproof clear plastic shield that takes up most of the legroom in the backseat of a New York City cab, then stayed there, hands, nose, lips and eyebrows pasted to the plastic as he looked through at this cabbie from Planet X, who, when finished ricocheting off his steering wheel, reached under his seat and came up with a shiny silver-and-black Glock machine pistol!

Yikes! There might not be much legroom back here, but Dortmunder found he could fit into it very well. He hit the deck, or the floor, shoulders and knees all meeting at his chin, and found himself wondering if that damn plastic actually was bulletproof after all.

Then he heard cracking and crashing sounds, like glass breaking, but when he stuck a quaking hand out, palm up, just beyond his quaking forehead, there were no bulletproof plastic pieces raining down. So what was being broken?

Unfolding himself from this position was much less easy, since he was much less motivated, but eventually he had his spine unpretzeled enough so he could peek through the bottom of the plastic shield just in time to watch the cabbie finish climbing through the windshield where he'd smashed out all the glass, and go rolling and scrambling over the hood to the street.

Dortmunder watched, and the guy got about four running steps down the street when his right leg just went out from under him and he cartwheeled in a spiral down to his right, flipping over like a surfer caught in the Big One, as the Glock went sailing straight up into the air, lazily turning, glinting in the light.

It was a weirdly beautiful scene, the Glock in the middle of the air. As it reached its apex, a uniformed cop stepped out from between two stopped vehicles, put his left hand out, and the Glock dropped into it like a trained parakeet. The cop grinned at the Glock, pleased with himself.

Now there were cops all over the place, just as in the recurrent nightmare Dortmunder had had for years, except none of these came floating down out of the sky. They gathered up the former cabbie, they directed traffic and then arranged for the garbage truck—which now had an interesting yellow speed stripe along its dark green side—to back up enough so they could open the right rear cab door and release the passenger.

Who knew he should not look reluctant to be rescued. It's OK if I seem shaky, he assured himself, and came out of the cab like a blender on steroids. "Th-thanks," he said, which he had never once said in that dream. "Th-thanks a lot."

"Man, you are lucky," one of the cops told him. "That is one of the major bombers and terrorists of all time. The *world* has been looking for that guy for years."

Dortmunder said, "And that's my luck? Today I hailed his cab?"

The cop asked, "Where'd you hail him?"

"In Brooklyn."

"And you brought him to Manhattan? That's great! We never would've found him in Brooklyn!"

All the cops were happy with Dortmunder for delivering this major league terrorist directly to the courthouse. They congratulated him and grinned at him and patted his shoulder and generally behaved in ways he was not used to from cops; it was disorienting.

Then one of them said, "Where were you headed?"

"West 78th Street."

A little discussion, and one of them said, "We'll go ahead and drive you the rest of the way."

In a police car? "No, no, that's OK," Dortmunder said.

"Least we can do," they said.

They insisted. When a cop insists, you go along. "OK, thanks," Dortmunder finally said.

"This way," a cop said.

They started down the street, now clogged with gawkers, and a cop behind Dortmunder yelled, "Hey!"

Oh, now what? Dortmunder turned, expecting the worst, and here came the cop, with the lunch bag in his hand. "You left this in the cab," he said.

"Oh," Dortmunder said. He was blinking a lot. "That's my lunch," he said. How could he have forgotten it?

"I figured," the cop said, and handed him the bag.

Dortmunder no longer trusted himself to speak. He nodded his thanks, turned away and shuffled after the cops who would drive him uptown.

Which they did. Fortunately, the conversation on the drive was all about the exploits of Kibam the terrorist—the name on the hack license was his own, backward—and not on the particulars of John Dortmunder.

Eventually they made the turn off Broadway onto 78th Street. Stoon lived in an apartment building in the middle of the block, so Dortmunder said, "Let me out anywhere along here."

"Sure," the cop driver said, and as he slowed Dortmunder looked out the window to see Stoon himself walking by, just as Stoon saw Dortmunder in the backseat of a slowing police car.

Stoon ran. Who wouldn't?

Knowing it was hopeless, but having to try, Dortmunder said, "Here's OK, this is fine, anywhere along here, this'd be good," while the cop driver just kept slowing and slowing, looking for a spot where there was a nice wide space between the parked cars, so his passenger would be able to get to the curb in comfort.

At last, stopped. Remembering his sandwich, knowing it was hopeless, unable to stop keeping on, Dortmunder said, "Thanks I appreciate it I really do this was terrific you guys have been—" until he managed to be outside and could slam the door.

But he couldn't run. Don't run away from a cop, it's worse than running away from a dog. He had to turn and walk, in stately fashion, rising on the balls of his feet, showing no urgency, no despair, not a care in the world, while the police car purred away down West 78th Street.

Broadway. Dortmunder turned the corner and looked up and down the street, and no Stoon. Of course not. Stoon would probably not come back to this neighborhood for a week. And the next time he saw Dortmunder, no matter what the circumstances, he'd run all over again, just on general principle.

Dortmunder sighed. There was nothing for it; he'd have to go see Arnie Albright.

Arnie Albright lived only eleven blocks away, on 89th between Broadway and West End. No more modes of transportation for today; Dortmunder didn't think his nerves could stand it. Holding tight to the lunch bag, he trekked up Broadway, and as he waited for the light to change at 79th Street a guy tapped him on the arm and said, "Excuse me. Is this your wallet?"

So here's the way it works. The scam artist has two identical wallets. The first one has a nice amount of cash in it, and ID giving a name and phone number. The scam artist approaches the mark, explains he just found this wallet on the sidewalk, and the two inspect it. They find a working pay phone—not always the easiest part of the scam—and call that phone number, and the "owner" answers and is overjoyed they found the wallet. If they wait right there, he'll come claim the wallet and give them a handsome reward (usually $100 to $500). The scam artist then explains he's late for an important appointment, and the mark should give him his half of the reward now ($50 to $250) and wait to collect from the owner. The mark hands over the money, the scam artist gives him the second wallet, the one with all the dollar-size pieces of newspaper in it, and the mark stands there on the corner awhile.

"Excuse me. Is this your wallet?"

Dortmunder looked at the wallet. "Yes," he said, plucked it out of the scam artist's hand, put it in his pocket and crossed 79th Street.

"Wait! Wait! Hey!"

On the north corner, the scam artist caught up and actually tugged at Dortmunder's sleeve. "Hey!" he said.

Dortmunder turned to look at him. "This is my wallet," he said. "You got a problem with that? You wanna call a cop? You want *me* to call a cop?"

The scam artist looked terribly, terribly hurt. He had beagle eyes. He looked as though he might cry. Dortmunder, a man with problems of his own, turned away and walked north to 89th Street and down the block to Arnie Albright's building, where he rang the bell in the vestibule.

"Now what?" snarled the intercom.

Dortmunder leaned close. He had never liked to say his own name out loud. "Dortmunder," he said.

"*Who?*"

"Cut it out, Arnie, you know who it is."

"Oh," the intercom yelled, "*Dortmunder!* Why didn't ya say so?"

The buzzer, a more pleasant sound than Arnie's voice, began its song, and Dortmunder pushed his way in and went up to

Arnie's apartment, where Arnie, a skinny, wiry ferret in charity cast-off clothing, stood in the doorway. "Dortmunder," he announced, "you look as crappy as I do."

Which could not be accurate. Dortmunder was having an eventful day, but nothing could make him look as bad as Arnie Albright, even normally, and when Dortmunder got a little closer he saw Arnie was at the moment even worse than normal. "What happened to *you?*" he asked.

"Nobody knows," Arnie said. "The lab says nobody's ever seen this in the temperate zones before. I look like the inside of a pomegranate."

This was true. Arnie, never a handsome specimen, now seemed to be covered by tiny red Vesuviuses, all of them oozing thin red salsa. In his left hand he held a formerly white hand towel, now wet and red, with which he kept patting his face and neck and forearms.

"Geez, Arnie, that's terrible," Dortmunder said. "How long you gonna have it? What's the doctor say?"

"Don't get too close to me."

"Don't worry, I won't."

"No, I mean that's what the doctor says. Now, you know and I know that nobody can stand me, on accounta my personality."

"Aw, no, Arnie," Dortmunder lied, though everybody in the world knew it was true. Arnie's personality, not his newly erupting volcanoes, were what had made him the last resort on Dortmunder's list of fences.

"Aw, yeah," Arnie insisted. "I rub people the wrong way. I argue with them, I'm obnoxious, I'm a pain in the ass. You wanna make something of it?"

"Not me, Arnie."

"But a doctor," Arnie said, "isn't supposed to like or not like. He's got that hypocritic oath. He's supposed to lie and pretend he likes you, and he's real glad he studied so hard in medical school so he could take care of nobody but *you*. But, no. My doctor says, 'Would you mind staying in the waiting room and just shout to me your symptoms?'"

"Huh," Dortmunder said.

"But what the hell do you care?" Arnie demanded. "You don't give a shit about me."

"Well," Dortmunder said.

"So if you're here, you scored, am I right?"

"Sure."

"Sure," Arnie said. "Why else would an important guy like you come to a turd like me? And so I also gotta understand Stoon's back in the jug, am I right?"

"No, you're wrong, Arnie," Dortmunder said. "Stoon's out. In fact, I just saw him jogging."

"Then how come you come to me?"

"He was jogging away from me," Dortmunder said.

"Well, what the hell, come on in," Arnie said, and got out of the doorway.

"Well, Arnie," Dortmunder said, "maybe we could talk it over out here."

"What, you think the apartment's contagious?"

"I'm just happy out here, that's all."

Arnie sighed, which meant that Dortmunder got a whiff of his breath. Stepping back a pace, he told him, "I got something."

"Or why would you be here. Let's see it."

Dortmunder took the paper towel–wrapped package out of the paper bag and dropped the bag on the floor. He unwrapped the paper towels and tucked them under his arm.

Arnie said, "What, are you delivering for a deli now? I'll give you a buck and half for it."

"Wait for it," Dortmunder advised. He dropped the top piece of Wonder Bread on the floor, along with much of the mayo and the top slab of ham. Using the paper towels, he lifted out the brooch, then dropped the rest of the sandwich on the floor and cleaned the brooch with the paper towels. Then he dropped the paper towels on the floor and held the brooch up so Arnie could see it, and said, "OK?"

"Oh, *you* got it," Arnie said. "I been seeing it on the news."

"In the *News*."

"On the news. The TV."

"Oh. Right."

"Let's have a look," Arnie said, and took a step forward.

Dortmunder took a step back. It had occurred to him that once Arnie had inspected this brooch, Dortmunder wouldn't be wanting it back. He said, "The newspaper says that it's worth $300,000."

"The newspaper says Dewey defeats Truman," Arnie said. "The newspaper says sunny, high in the 70s. The newspaper says informed sources report. The news—"

"OK, OK. But I just wanna be sure we're gonna come to an agreement here."

"Dortmunder," Arnie said, "you know me. Maybe you don't *want* to know me, but you know me. I give top dollar, I don't cheat, I am 100 percent reliable. I don't act like a normal guy and cheat and gouge, because if I did, nobody would ever come to see me at all. I have to be a saint, because I'm such a shit. Toss it over."

"OK," Dortmunder said, and tossed it over, and Arnie caught it in his revolting towel. Whatever he offers, I'll take, Dortmunder thought.

While Arnie studied the brooch, breathing on it, turning it, Dortmunder looked in his new wallet and saw it contained a little over $300 cash, plus the usual ID plus a lottery ticket. The faking of the numbers on the lottery ticket was pretty well done. So that would have been the juice in the scam.

"Well," Arnie said, "these diamonds are not diamonds. They're glass."

"Glass? You mean somebody conned the movie star?"

"I know that couldn't happen," Arnie agreed, "and yet it did. And this silver isn't silver, it's plate."

In his heart, Dortmunder had known it would be like this. All this effort, and zip. "And the green things?" he said.

Arnie looked at him in surprise. "They're emeralds," he said. "Don't you know what emeralds look like?"

"I thought I did," Dortmunder said. "So it's worth something, after all."

"Not the way it is," Arnie said. "Not with its picture all over the news. And not with the diamonds and silver being nothing but shit. Somebody's gotta pop the emeralds out, throw away the rest of it, sell the emeralds by themself."

"For what?"

"I figure they might go for 40 apiece," Arnie said. "But there's the cost of popping them."

"Arnie," Dortmunder said, "what are we talking here?"

Arnie said, "I could go seven. You wanna try around town, nobody else is gonna give you more than five, if they even want the hassle. You got a famous thing here."

Seven. He'd dreamed of 30, he would have been happy with 25. Seven. "I'll take it," Dortmunder said.

Arnie said, "But not today."

"Not today?"

"Look at me," Arnie said. "You want me to hand you something?"

"Well, no."

"I owe you seven," Arnie said. "If this shit I got don't kill me, I'll pay you when I can touch things. I'll phone you."

A promissory note—not even a note, nothing in writing—from a guy oozing salsa. "OK, Arnie," Dortmunder said. "Get well soon, you know?"

Arnie looked at his own forearms. "Maybe what it is," he said, "is my personality coming out. Maybe when it's over I'll be a completely different guy. Whaddya think?"

"Don't count on it," Dortmunder told him.

Well, at least he had the $300 from the wallet scam. And maybe Arnie would live; he certainly *seemed* too mean to die.

Heading back to Broadway, Dortmunder started the long walk downtown—no more things on wheels, not today—and at 86th Street he saw that a new edition of the *New York Post* was prominent on the newsstand on the corner. JER-FELICIA SPLIT was the front-page headline. That, apparently, in the *New York Post*'s estimation, was the most important North American news since the last time Donald Trump had it on or off with somebody or other.

What the hell; Dortmunder could splurge. He had $300 and a promise. He bought the paper, just to see what had happened to the formerly loving couple.

He had happened, essentially. The loss of the pin (brioche, brooch) had hit the lovers hard. "It's in diversity you really get to know another person," Felicia was reported as saying, with a side-bar in which a number of resident experts fron NYU, Columbia and Fordham agreed, tentatively, that when Felicia had said diversity she had actually meant adversity.

"I remain married to my muse," Jer was quoted as announcing. "It's back to the studio to make another film for my public." No experts were felt to be needed to explicate that statement.

Summing it all up, the *Post* reporter finished his piece, "The double-emerald brooch may be worth $300,000, but no one seems to have found much happiness in it." I know what you mean, Dortmunder thought, and walked home.

ART AND CRAFT

THE VOICE ON THE TELEPHONE AT JOHN DORTMUNDER'S EAR didn't so much as ring a distant bell as sound a distant siren. "John," it rasped, "how ya doin'?"

Better before this phone call, Dortmunder thought. Somebody I was in prison with, he figured, but who? He'd been in prison with so many people, back before he had learned how to fade into the shadows at crucial moments, like when the SWAT team arrives. And of all those cellmates, blockmates, tankmates, there hadn't been one of them who wasn't there for some very good reason. DNA would never stumble over innocence in that crowd; the best DNA could do for those guys was find their fathers, if that's what they wanted.

This wasn't a group that went in for reunions, so why this phone call, in the middle of the day, in the middle of the week, in the middle of October? "I'm doin' OK," Dortmunder answered, meaning, I got enough cash for me but not enough for you.

"That makes two of us," the voice said. "In case you don't recognize me, this is Three Finger."

"Oh," Dortmunder said.

Three Finger Gillie possessed the usual 10 fingers but got his name because of a certain fighting technique. Fights in prison tend to be up close and personal, and also brief; Three Finger had a move with three fingers of his right hand guaranteed to make the other guy rethink his point of view in a hurry. Dortmunder had always stayed more than an arm's reach from Three Finger and saw no reason to change that policy. "I guess you're out, huh?" he said.

Sounding surprised, Three Finger said, "You didn't read about me in the paper?"

"Oh, too bad," Dortmunder said, because in their world the worst thing that could happen was to find your name in the paper. Indictment was bad enough, but to be indicted for something newsworthy was the worst.

But Three Finger said, "Naw, John, this is good. This is what we call ink."

"Ink."

"You still got last Sunday's *Times*?" he asked.

Astonished, Dortmunder said, "*The New York Times?*"

"Sure, what else? 'Arts and Leisure,' page 14, check it out, and then we'll make a meet. How about tomorrow, four o'clock?"

"A meet. You got something on?"

"Believe it. You know Portobello?"

"What is that, a town?"

"Well, it's a mushroom, but it's also a terrific little cafe on Mercer Street. You ought to know it, John."

"OK," Dortmunder said.

"Four o'clock tomorrow."

Keeping one's distance from Three Finger Gillie was always a good idea, but on the other hand he had Dortmunder's phone number, so he probably had his address as well, and he was known to be a guy who held a grudge. Squeezed it, in fact. "See you there," Dortmunder promised, and went away to see if he knew anybody who might own a last Sunday's *New York Times.*

* * *

The dry cleaner on Third Avenue had a copy.

Life is very different for Martin Gillie these days. "A big improvement," he says in his gravelly voice, and laughs as he picks up his mocha cappuccino.

And indeed life is much improved for this longtime state prison inmate with a history of violence. For years, Gillie was considered beyond any hope of rehabilitation, but then the nearly impossible came to pass. "Other guys find religion in the joint," he explains, "but I found art."

It was a period of solitary confinement brought about by his assault on a fellow inmate that led Gillie to try his hand at drawing, first with stubs of pencils on magazine pages, then with crayons on typewriter paper, and, finally, when his work drew the appreciative attention of prison authorities, with oil on canvas.

These last artworks, allegorical treatments of imaginary cityscapes, led to Gillie's appearance in several group shows. They also led to his parole (his having been turned down three previous times), and now his first solo show, in Soho's Waspail Gallery.

Dortmunder read through to the end, disbelieving but forced to believe. *The New York Times;* the newspaper with a record, right? So it had to be true.

"Thanks," he told the dry cleaner, and walked away, shaking his head.

Among the nymphs and ferns of Portobello, Three Finger Gillie looked like the creature that gives fairy tales their tension. A burly man with thick black hair that curled low on his forehead and lapped over his ears and collar, he also featured a single, wide block of black eyebrow like a weight holding his eyes down. These eyes were pale blue and squinty and not warm, and they peered suspiciously out from both sides of a bumpy nose shaped like a baseball left out in the rain. The mouth, what there was of it, was thin and straight and without color. Dortmunder had never before seen this head above anything but prison denim, so it was a surprise to see it chunked down on top of a black cashmere turtleneck sweater and a maroon vinyl jacket with the zipper open. Dressed like this, Gillie mostly gave the impression he'd stolen his body from an off-duty cop.

Looking at him, seated there, with a fancy coffee cup in front of him—mocha cappuccino?—Dortmunder remembered that other surprise, from the newspaper, that Three Finger had another front name. Martin. Crossing the half-empty restaurant, weighing the alternatives, he came to the conclusion no. Not a Martin. This was still a Three Finger.

He didn't rise as Dortmunder approached, but patted his palm on the white marble table as if to say siddown. Dortmunder pulled out the delicate black wrought-iron chair, said, "You look the same, Three Finger," and sat.

"And yet," Three Finger said, "on the inside I'm all changed. You're the same as ever outside and in, aren't you?"

"Probably," Dortmunder agreed. "I read that thing in the paper."

"Ink," Three Finger reminded him, and smiled, showing the same old hard, gray, uneven teeth. "It's publicity, John," he said, "that runs the art world. It don't matter, you could be a genius, you could be Da Vinci, you don't know how to publicize yourself, forget it."

"I guess you must know, then," Dortmunder said.

"Well, not enough," Three Finger admitted. "The show's been open since last Thursday, a whole week. I'm only up three weeks, we got two red dots."

Dortmunder said, "Do that again," and here came the willowy waitress, wafting over with a menu that turned out to be eight pages of coffee. When Dortmunder found regular American, with cream and sugar—page five—she went away and Three Finger said, "Up, when I say I'm only up three weeks, I mean that's how long my show is, then they take my stuff down off the walls and put somebody else up. And when I say two red dots, the way they work it, when somebody buys a picture, they don't get to take it home right away, not till the show's over, so the gallery puts a red dot next to the name on the wall, everybody knows it's sold. In a week, I got two red dots."

"And that's not so good, huh?"

"I got 43 canvases up there, John," Three Finger said. "This racket is supposed to keep me out of jewelry stores after hours. I gotta have more than two red dots."

"Gee, I wish you well," Dortmunder said.

"Well, you can do better than that," Three Finger told him. "That's why I called you."

Here it comes, Dortmunder thought. He wants me to buy a painting. I never thought anybody I knew in the whole world would ever want me to buy a painting. How do I get out of this?

But what Three Finger said next was another surprise: "What you can do for me, you can rip me off."

"Ha-ha," Dortmunder said.

"No, listen to me, John," Three Finger said. Leaning close over the marble table, dangerously within arm's reach, lowering his voice and peering intensely out of those icy eyes, he said, "This world we're in, John, this is a world of irony."

Dortmunder had been lost since yesterday, when he'd read the piece in the newspaper, and nothing that was happening today was making him any more found. "Oh, yeah?" he said.

Three Finger lifted both hands above his head—Dortmunder flinched, but only a little—and made quotation signs. "Everything's in quotes," he said. "Everybody's taking a step back, looking the situation over, being cool."

"Uh-huh," Dortmunder said.

"Now, I got some ink," Three Finger went on. "I already got

some, but it isn't enough. The ex-con is an artist, this has some ironic interest in it, but what we got here, we got a situation where everybody's got some ironic interest in them, everybody's got some edge, some attitude. I gotta call attention to myself. More ironic than thou, you see what I mean?"

"Sure," Dortmunder lied.

"So, what if the ex-con artist gets robbed?" Three Finger wanted to know. "The gallery gets burgled, you see what I mean?"

"Not entirely," Dortmunder admitted.

"A burglary doesn't get into the papers," Three Finger pointed out. "A burglary isn't news. A burglary is just another fact of life, like a fender bender."

"Sure."

"But if you give it that ironic edge," Three Finger said, low and passionate, "then it's the edge that gets in the paper gets on TV. That's what gets me on the talk shows. Not the ex-con turned artist, that isn't enough. Not some penny-ante burglary, nobody cares. But the ex-con turned artist gets ripped off, his old life returns to bite him on the ass, what he used to be rises up and slaps him on the face. Now you've got your irony. Now I can get this sheepish kinda grin on my face, and I can say, 'Gee, Oprah, I guess in a funny way this is the dues I'm paying,' and I got 43 red dots on the wall, you see what I mean?"

"Maybe," Dortmunder allowed, but it was hard to think this way. Publicity was to him pretty much what fire was to the Scarecrow in Oz. There was no way that he could possibly look on public exposure as a good thing. But if that's where Three Finger was right now, reversing a lifetime of ingrained behavior, shifting from a skulk to a strut, fine.

However, that left one question, so Dortmunder asked it: "What's in it for me?"

Three Finger looked surprised. "The insurance money," he said.

"What, you get it and you split it with me?"

"No, no, art theft doesn't work like that." Three Finger reached into the inside pocket of his jacket—Dortmunder flinched, but barely—and brought out a business card. Sliding it across the marble table, he said, "This is the agent for the gallery's insurance company. The way it works, you go in, you grab as many as you want—leave the red dot ones alone, that's all I ask—then you call the agent, you dicker a fee to return the stuff. Somewhere between maybe 10 and 25 percent."

"And I just walk back in with these paintings," Dortmunder said, "and nobody arrests me."

"You don't walk back in," Three Finger told him. "Come on, John, you're a pro, that's why I called you. It's like a kidnapping, you do it the same way. You can figure that part out. The insurance company wants to pay you because they'd have to pay the gallery a whole lot more."

Dortmunder said, "And what's the split?"

"Nothing, John," Three Finger said. "The money's all yours. Don't worry, I'll make out. You hit that gallery in the next week, I get ink. Believe me, where I am now, ink is better than money."

"Then you're in some funny place," Dortmunder told him.

"It's a lot better than where I used to be, John," Three Finger said.

Dortmunder picked up the business card and looked at it, and the willowy waitress brought him coffee in a round mauve cup the size of Elmira, so he put the card in his pocket. When she went away, he said, "I'll think about it." Because what else would he do?

"You could go there today," Three Finger said. "Not with me, you know."

"Sure."

"You case the joint, if it looks good, you do it. The place closes at seven, you do it between eight and midnight, any night at all. I'm guaranteed to be with a crowd, so nobody thinks I ripped myself off for the publicity stunt."

Three Finger reached into his jacket again—Dortmunder did not flinch a bit—and brought out a postcard with a shiny picture on one side. Sliding it across the table, he said, "This is like my calling card these days. The gallery address is on the other side."

It was a reproduction of a painting, one of Three Finger's, had to be. Dortmunder picked it up by the edges because the picture covered the whole area, and looked at a nighttime street scene. A side street, with a bar and some brick tenements and parked cars. It wasn't dark, but the light was a little weird, streetlights and bar lights and lights in windows, all a little too green or a little too blue. No people showed anywhere along the street or in the windows, but you just had a feeling there were people there, barely out of sight, hiding maybe in a doorway, behind a car. It wasn't a neighborhood you'd want to stay in.

"Keep it," Three Finger said. "I got a stack of 'em."

Dortmunder pocketed the card, thinking he'd show it to his faithful companion this evening and she'd tell him what to think about it. "I'll give the place the double-O," he promised.

"I can't ask more," Three Finger assured him.

The neighborhood had been full of lofts and warehouses and light manufacturing. Then commerce left, went over to New Jersey or out to the Island, and the artists moved in, for the large spaces at low rents. But the artists made it trendy, so the real estate people moved in, changed the name to Soho, which in London does not mean South of Houston Street, and the rents went through the roof. The artists had to move out, but they left their paintings behind, in the new galleries. Parts of Soho still look pretty much like before, but some of it has been touristed up so much it doesn't look like New York City at all. It looks like Charlotte Amalie, on a dimmer.

The Waspail Gallery was in a little cluster that had been touristed. In the first place, it came with its own parking lot. In New York?

A U of buildings, half a block's worth, had been taken over for a series of shops and cafes. The most beat-up of the original buildings had been knocked down to make access to the former backyards, which were blacktopped into a parking area, plus selling and eating space. The shops and cafes faced out onto the three streets surrounding the U; and they all also had entrances in back, from the parking lot.

The Waspail Gallery was midway down the left arm of the U. The original of the postcard in Dortmunder's pocket stood on an easel in the big front window, looking even more menacing at life size. Inside, a stainless-steel girl in black presided at a little cherrywood desk, while three browsers browsed in the background. The girl gave Dortmunder one appraising look, glanced outside to see if it was raining, decided there was no telling and went back to her *Interview.*

All the pictures were early evening or night scenes of city streets, never with any people, always with that sense of hidden menace. Some were bigger, some were smaller, all had weirdness in the lighting. Dortmunder found the two with red dots—*Scheme* and *Before the Rain*—and they were the same as all the others. How could you tell you wanted this one and not that one over there?

Dortmunder browsed among the browsers, but mostly he was browsing for security. He saw the alarm system over the front door, a make and model he'd amused himself with in the past, and he smiled it a hello. He saw the locks on the doors at front and back, he saw the solid sheet metal–articulated gate that would ratchet down over the front window at night to protect the glass and to keep passersby from seeing any burglar who might happen to be inside, and eventually he saw the thick iron mesh on the small window in the unisex bathroom.

What he didn't see was the surveillance camera. A joint with this alarm and those locks and that gate would usually have a surveillance camera, either to videotape with a motion sensor or to take still pictures every minute or so. So where was it?

There. Tucked away inside an apparent heating system grid

high on the right wall. Dortmunder caught a glimpse of light reflecting off the lens, and it wasn't until the next time he browsed by that he could figure out which way it pointed—diagonally toward the front entrance. So a person coming in from the back could avoid it without a problem.

He went out the back way, past the tourists snacking at tables on the asphalt, and home.

He didn't like it. He wasn't sure what it was, but something was wrong. He would have gone in and lifted a few pictures that first night, if he'd felt comfortable about it, but he didn't. Something was wrong.

Was it just that this was connected with Three Finger Gillie, from whom nothing good had ever flowed? Or was there something else that he just couldn't put his finger on?

It wasn't the money. Gillie didn't plan to rip off Dortmunder later on, or he'd have agreed to share the pie from the get-go. It was the publicity he wanted. And Dortmunder didn't believe Gillie meant to double-cross him, turn him in to get himself some extra publicity, because it would be too easy to show they used to know each other in the old days, and Gillie's being the inside man in the boost would be obvious.

No, it wasn't Gillie himself, at least not directly. It was something else that didn't feel right, something having to do with that gallery.

Of course, he could just forget the whole thing, take a walk. He didn't owe Three Finger Gillie any favors. But if there was something wrong, was it a smart idea to walk away without at least finding out what was what?

The third day, Dortmunder decided to go back to the gallery one more time, see if he could figure out what was bugging him.

This time, he thought he'd walk in the parking entrance and go into the gallery from that side, to see what it felt like. The first thing he saw, at an outdoor cafe across the half-empty lot from the gallery, was Jim O'Hara, drinking a Diet Pepsi. At least, the cup was a Diet Pepsi cup.

Jim O'Hara. A coincidence?

O'Hara was a guy Dortmunder had worked with here and there, around and about, from time to time. They'd done some things together. However, they didn't travel in the same circles on a regular basis, so how did it happen that Jim O'Hara was here, and not looking at the rear entrance to the Waspail Gallery?

Dortmunder walked down the left side of the parking area, past the gallery (without looking at it), and when he was sure he'd caught O'Hara's attention, he stopped, nodded as though he'd just decided on something, turned around and walked back out to the street.

The remaining parts of the original Soho neighborhood included some bars. Dortmunder found one after a three-block walk, purchased a draft beer, took it to a booth and had sipped twice before O'Hara joined him, having traded his Diet Pepsi for a draft of his own. For greeting, he said, "He talked to you, too, huh?"

"Three days ago," Dortmunder said. "When'd he talk to you?"

"Forty minutes ago. He'll talk until somebody does it, I guess. How come you didn't?"

"Smelled wrong," Dortmunder said.

O'Hara nodded. "Me, too. That's why I was sitting there, trying to figure it out."

Dortmunder said, "Who knows how many people he's telling the story to."

"So we walk away from it."

"No, we can't," Dortmunder told him. "That's what I finally realized when I saw you sitting over there."

O'Hara drank beer, and frowned. "Why can't we just forget it?"

"The whole thing hangs together," Dortmunder said. "What got to me, in that gallery there, and now I know it, and it's the answer to what's wrong with this picture, is the security camera."

"What security camera?" O'Hara asked, and then said, "You're right, there should have been one, and there wasn't."

"Well, there was," Dortmunder told him. "Tucked away in a vent thing on the wall. But the thing about a security camera, it's always right out there, mounted under the ceiling, out where you can see it. That's part of the security, that you're supposed to know it's there."

"Why, that son of a bitch," O'Hara said.

"Oops, wait a minute, I know that fella," O'Hara said the next night, back in the gallery-facing parking lot. "Be right back."

"I'll be here," Dortmunder said as O'Hara rose to intercept an almost invisible guy approaching the gallery across the way, a skinny slinking guy in dark gray jacket, dark gray pants, black sneakers and black baseball cap worn frontward.

Dortmunder watched the two not quite meet and then leave the parking area not quite together, and then for a while he watched tourists yawn at the tables around him until O'Hara and the other guy walked back together. They came to the table and O'Hara said, "Pete, John. John, Pete."

"Harya."

"That Three Finger's something, isn't he?" Pete said, and sat with them. Then he smiled up at the actor turned waiter who materialized before him like a genie out of a bottle. "Nothing for me, thanks, pal," Pete said. "I'm up to here in Chicken McNuggets."

The actor shrugged and vanished, while Dortmunder decided not to ask for a definition of Chicken McNuggets. Instead, he said, "It was today he talked to you?"

"Yeah, and I was gonna do it, that's how bright I am," Pete said. "Like the fella says, I get along with a little help from my friends, without whom I'd be asking for my old cell back."

O'Hara said, "Happy to oblige." To Dortmunder he said, "Pete agrees with us."

Pete said, "And it's tonight, am I right?"

"Before he recruits an entire platoon," Dortmunder said.

O'Hara said, "Or before somebody actually does it."

For a second, it looked as though Pete might offer to shake hands all around. But he quelled that impulse, grinned at them instead and said, "Like the fella says, all for one and one for all and a sharp stick in the eye for Three Finger."

"Hear, hear," O'Hara said.

Three-fifteen in the morning. While O'Hara and Dortmunder waited in the car they'd borrowed out in Queens earlier this evening, Pete slithered along the storefronts toward the parking area entrance at the far end of the block. Halfway there, he disappeared into the shifting shadows of the night.

"He moves nice," Dortmunder said in approval.

"Uh-huh," O'Hara said. "Pete's never paid to see a movie in his life."

They waited about five minutes, and then Pete appeared again, having to come almost all the way back to the car before he could catch their attention. In that time, a couple of cruising cabs had gone by on the wider cross-streets ahead and behind, but nothing at all had moved on this block.

"Here's Pete now," O'Hara said, and they got out of the car and followed him back down to the parking area's gates, which were kept locked at night, except for now. Along the way, speaking in a gray murmur, O'Hara asked, "Any trouble?"

"Easy," Pete murmured back. "Not as easy as if I could bust things up, but easy."

Pete had not, in fact, busted anything up. The gates looked as solidly locked as ever, completely untampered with, but when Pete gave a small push they swung right out of the way. The trio stepped through, Pete closed the gates again and here they were.

Dortmunder looked around, and at night, with nobody here, this parking area surrounded by shut shops looked just like Three

Finger's paintings. Even the security lights in the stores were a little strange, a little too white or a little too pink. It was spooky.

They'd agreed that Dortmunder, as the one who'd caught on to the scam, had his choice of jobs here tonight, and he'd picked the art gallery. It would be more work than the other stuff, more delicate, but it would also be more personal and therefore more satisfying. So the three split up, and Dortmunder approached the gallery, first putting on a pair of thin rubber gloves, then taking a roll of keys from his pocket. The other two, meantime, who were also now gloved, were taking pry bars and chisels from their pockets as they neared a pair of other shops.

Dortmunder worked slowly and painstakingly. He wasn't worried about the locks or the alarm system; they were nothing to get into a sweat over. But the point here was to do the job without leaving any traces, the way Pete had done the gate.

The other two didn't have such problems. Breaking into stores, the only thing they had to be careful about was making too much noise, since there were apartments on the upper floors here, among the chiropractors and psychic readers. But within that limitation, they made no attempt at all to be neat or discreet. Every shop door was mangled. Inside the shops, they peeled the faces off safes, they gouged open cash register tills and they left interior doors sagging from their hinges.

Every shop in the compound was hit, the costume jewelry store and the souvenir shop and the movie memorabilia place and both antique shops and the fine-leather store and both cafes and the other art gallery. They didn't get a lot from any one of these places, but they got something from each.

Dortmunder meanwhile had gained access to the Waspail Gallery. Taking the stainless-steel girl's chair from the cherry-wood table, he carried it over to the grid in the wall concealing the security camera, climbed up on the chair and carefully unscrewed the grid, being sure not to leave any scratches. The grid was hinged at the bottom; he lowered it to the wall, looked inside, and the camera looked back at him. A motion sensor machine, it had sensed motion and was now humming quietly to itself as it took Dortmunder's picture.

That's OK, Dortmunder thought, enjoy yourself. While you can.

The space was a small oblong box built into the wall, larger than a shoebox but smaller than a liquor store carton. An electric outlet was built into its right side, with the camera plugged into it. Dortmunder reached past the lens, pulled the plug and the camera stopped humming. Then he figured out how to move this widget forward on the right side of the mounting—*tick*—and the camera lifted right off.

He brought the camera down and placed it on the floor, then climbed back up on the chair to put the grid in its original place. Certain he'd left no marks on it, he climbed down, put the chair where it belonged and wiped its seat with his sleeve.

Next, the tapes. There would be tapes from this camera, probably two a day. Where would they be?

The cherrywood table's drawer was locked, and that took a while, leaving no marks, and then the tapes weren't there. A closet was also locked and also took a little while, and turned out to be full of brooms and toilet paper and a bunch of things like that. A storeroom was locked, which by now Dortmunder found irritating, and inside it were some folding chairs and a folding table and general party supplies and a ladder, and stuff like that, and a tall metal locker, and that was locked.

All right, all right, it's all good practice. And inside the metal locker were 12 tapes. At last. Dortmunder brought out from one of his many jacket pockets a plastic bag from the supermarket, into which went the tapes. Then he locked his way back out of the locker and the storeroom, and added the camera to the plastic bag. Then he locked his way out of the gallery, and there were O'Hara and Pete, in a pool of shadow, carrying their own full plastic bags, waiting for him.

"Took you a while," O'Hara said.

Dortmunder didn't like to be criticized. "I had to find the tapes," he said.

"As the fella says, time well spent," Pete assured him.

Dortmunder's faithful companion, May, came home from her cashier's job at the supermarket the next evening to say, "That fellow you told me about, that Martin Gillie, he's in the newspaper." By which, of course, she meant the *Daily News*.

"That's called ink," Dortmunder informed her.

"I don't think so," she said, and handed him the paper. "This time, I think it's called felony arrest."

Dortmunder smiled at the glowering face of Three Finger Gillie on page five of the *News*. He didn't have to read the story, he knew what it had to say.

May watched him. "John? Did you have something to do with that?"

"A little," he said. "See, May, when he told me that all he wanted was publicity, it was the truth. It was a stretch for Three Finger to tell the truth, but he pulled it off. But his idea was, every day he talks another ex-con into walking through that gallery, looking it over for maybe a burglary. He's going to do that every day until one of those guys actually robs the place. Then he's going to show what a reformed character he is by volunteering to look at the surveillance tapes. 'Oh, there's a guy I used to know!' he'll say, feigning surprise. 'And there's another one. They must of all been in it together.' Then the cops roust us all, and one of us actually does have the stolen paintings, so we're all accomplices, so we all go upstate forever, and there's steady publicity for Three Finger, all through the trials and the appeals, and he's this poster boy for rehabilitation, and he's got ink, he's on television day and night, he's famous, he's successful, and we probably deserved to go upstate anyway."

"What a rat," May said.

"You know it," Dortmunder agreed. "So we couldn't just walk away, because we're on those tapes, and we don't know when somebody else is gonna pull the job. So if we have to go in, get the tapes, we might as well make some profit out of it. And give a little zing to Three Finger while we're at it."

"They decided it was him pretty fast," she said.

"His place was the only one not hit," Dortmunder pointed out to May. "So it looks like the rehabilitation didn't take after all, that he just couldn't resist temptation."

"I suppose," she said.

"Also," he said, "you remember that little postcard with his painting that I showed you but I wouldn't let you touch?"

"Sure. So?"

"Myself," Dortmunder said, "I only held it by the edges, just in case. The last thing we did last night, I dropped that postcard on the floor in front of the cash register in the leather store. With his fingerprints all over it. His calling card, he said it was."

In the introduction to this volume, I recorded that bleak period of time, some years ago, when it looked as though I might lose the rights to John Dortmunder's name to marauding bands of Hollywood lawyers. Fortunately, that threat did eventually recede, but before that happy deliverance I'd settled on a substitute name for John, in case he should have to go underground for a while and come back under an alias, with fake ID. That name, found after an extensive search and taken from an exit sign on the Saw Mill River Parkway in Westchester County, just north of New York City, was John Rumsey.

The only problem, I soon realized, is that John Rumsey is a shorter person than John Dortmunder; don't ask me why. Dortmunder's, oh, say, an even six foot. John Rumsey's five seven at best.

From time to time, I wondered if Rumsey would be different in any other ways, not through my conscious choice, but simply because of the changed indicator. And what about the other regulars in his crew? I didn't have to know the answer to that, happily, but the question just kept poking at me.

In assembling this volume, I realized that if I were to add just one more story, I could use the present title for the book. I'd had a story title, "Fugue for Felons," in mind for some time, and now I saw how it would play out, and also that it would be a great laboratory. Here was my chance for an experiment to solve that age-old question: What's in a name?

A lot, as it turns out. Halfway through writing the story, I realized it wasn't an experiment that could be reversed or undone. I couldn't simply put the original names back on the name tags, because these weren't the original people. In small but crucial ways, they were their own men. John Rumsey was not John Dortmunder, and not merely because he was shorter. Similarly, Algy was not Andy Kelp, Big Hooper was not Tiny Bulcher, and Stan Little was not Stan

Murch. ("Murch," it turns out, is an obsolete medieval term for "dwarf," which I hadn't known until I looked in the OED in conjunction with writing the story.)

Names are important. And so, although "Fugue for Felons" is the most recent Dortmunder story, it is also not a Dortmunder story at all. In some parallel universe, where the sky is a little paler, the streets a little cleaner, the laws of probability a little chancier, where the roses don't smell quite the same, there exist John Rumsey and his friends, the closest that other cosmos can come to Dortmunder et al. And now I have visited them.

FUGUE FOR FELONS

JOHN RUMSEY, A SHORT BLUNT MAN WITH THE LOOK OF A ONE-time contender about him, was eating his breakfast—maple syrup garnished with French toast—when his faithful companion June looked up from her *Daily News* to say, "Isn't Morry Calhoun a friend of yours?"

"I know him," Rumsey admitted; that far he was willing to go.

"Well, they arrested him," June said.

"He made the paper?" In Rumsey's world, there was nothing worse than reading your own name in the newspaper, particularly the *Daily News*, which all one's friends also read.

"It's a little piece," June said, "but there's a picture of the car in the bank, and then his name caught my eye."

"The car *in* the bank?"

"Police," June told him, "came across Morry Calhoun last night, breaking into the Flatbush branch of Immigration Trust. A high-speed chase from Brooklyn to Queens ended when Calhoun crashed his car into the Sunnyside branch of Immigration Trust."

"Well, he's got brand loyalty anyway," Rumsey said.

"They're holding him without bail," June went on.

"Yeah, they do that," agreed Rumsey. "It's kind of an honor, in a way, but it's also confining. There's a picture of this car in this bank?"

June passed the paper over her plate of dry toast and his bowl of wet syrup, and Rumsey looked at a picture of the ass end of an Infiniti sticking out of the front of a branch bank that had been mostly glass until Calhoun arrived.

"The car was stolen," June said.

"Sure, it would be," Rumsey said, and squinted at the photo. "Bank's closed."

"Naturally," June said. "Until they fix the front."

"You know," Rumsey said, "it might be a good idea, wander out there, see is there anything lying around."

"Don't get in trouble," June advised.

"Me? I'll just call Algy," Rumsey decided, getting to his feet, "see would he like to take a train ride."

But there was no answer at Algy's place.

Algy, in fact, a skinny sharp-nosed guy, was already on the subway, heading back toward Manhattan from Queens after a night of very little success at breaking and entering. He'd broken, all right, and he'd entered, but everywhere he went, the occupant had just moved out, or had a dog, or didn't have anything at all. It could be a discouragement at times.

About the only thing Algy scored, in fact, other than half a liverwurst on rye in Saran Wrap in a refrigerator in Queens, was a *Daily News* some other passenger had left behind on the seat. He glanced through it, saw the picture of the car in the bank, recognized Morry Calhoun's name, got off at the next stop, and took the first train going the other way.

Big Hooper was called Big because he was *big*. You could say he looked like an elephant in sweats, or an Easter Island statue no longer buried up to the neck, but what he mostly looked like was the Chicago Bears front line—not a lineman, the line.

Big Hooper had just bent to his will the front door of a Third Avenue tavern not yet open for business, intending to give himself a morning vodka-and-Chianti before carrying away the cash register, when he realized he wasn't alone. The clinking and tinking from the back room suggested the owner was using this morning downtime to do inventory, having left his jacket and newspaper on the bar.

Big went ahead and made his breakfast, then leafed through the paper while trying to decide whether to deal with the jangling offstage owner or come back another time, when he could have some privacy. He saw the Infiniti impaled on the bank, recognized the name Calhoun, finished his drink, and left. He took the paper.

Stan Little was a driver. If you've got it, he'll drive it. When he wasn't working for various crews around town on their little errands, sometimes he drove for himself, picking up an example of your better-quality automotive cream puff and tooling it to Astoria in Queens, where he would have business dealings with Al Gonzo, an automotive importer-exporter, who would eventually find the merchandise a good home somewhere in the Third World. This morning, while discussing with Al the probable offshore value of a loaded Saab with less than three K on the odometer, Stan took the opportunity of Al's strategic long silences to eyeball the *Daily News*.

"All right, four," Al said.

"Well, look at that," Stan said. "Morry Calhoun."

The reason Rumsey got off the F train early was because two transit cops went through his car and they both looked at him funny. Rumsey didn't like cops to look at him at all, much less funny, so he quick got off at the next station, even though it wasn't his but was in fact Queens Plaza, which is one of those giant bow ties in the bowels of the New York City subway system.

There are 24 separate subway lines in New York, and four of them converge on Queens Plaza, distributing thousands and thousands of people this way and that every second. There's the F, the 6th Avenue local that Rumsey had been on, which begins in nethermost Brooklyn, wanders northward to run under 6th Avenue in Manhattan, then heads on to outermost Queens; the R, the Broadway local, which is similar except its part of Manhattan is lower Broadway; the 8th Avenue E, which only has to deal with Manhattan and Queens; and the poor G, the Brooklyn Queens Crosstown, which never gets into Manhattan at all but just shuttles back and forth between Brooklyn and Queens, full of people wearing hats.

Having got off the F, there was nothing for Rumsey to do but wait for another F, or some other letter, and so continue his journey in peace, but lo and behold, here were two more transit cops, and now *they* were looking at him funny. Maybe, he thought, he'd take the escalator upstairs to where the surface part of the bow tie was a lot of bus routes starting with "Q," but as he turned away, with millions of people rushing all around him in this great echoing iron cavern, this paean to 19th-century engineering at its sternest, a voice cut through the din and the roar to say, "You. Yeah, you. Wait there."

Now the cops were *talking* to him; this was very bad. Feeling guilty, even though he hadn't committed any crimes yet today, Rumsey turned about, hunched his shoulders in that automatic way that tells police officers everywhere that you *are* guilty, and said, "Me?"

It is impossible for two human beings to completely surround one human being, and yet these two cops did it. They were big bulky guys with big dark bulky uniforms festooned with serious extras like a gun in a holster and a ticket book and handcuffs (Rumsey didn't like to look at handcuffs) and a little black radio fastened up high on the black belt that angled down across their chests. Their very presence said *authority*; it said *you're in for it now, Jack*; it said *fuggedaboudit*.

"See s' ID," one of the cops said.

"Oh, sure," Rumsey said, because, no matter what, you never

disagree when authority is this close into your personal space. He remembered he'd packed somebody's ID when he'd left the house, so he went to his hip pocket for his wallet, while the cops watched him very carefully, and as he handed over somebody's credit card and the same somebody's library card from the branch in Canarsie, he said, "Uh, what's the problem, officers?"

The cop who took the ID said, "How about your driver's license?"

"They took my license," Rumsey explained. "Just temporary, you know."

The other cop chuckled. "You were a bad boy, huh?"

That was cop humor. Rumsey acknowledged it with a sheepish grin, saying, "I guess so. But what's wrong here?"

The cop with the ID said, "We're looking for a guy, Mr. Jefferson."

So he was Mr. Jefferson today. Trying to feel Jeffersonian, Rumsey said, "Well, why pick me? There's a lotta guys here." Millions, in fact—on escalators, in subway trains, on platforms . . .

"The description we got," the humorous cop said, "looks like you."

"A lotta guys look like me," Rumsey said.

"Not really," the cop said, and all at once their two radios squawked, making Rumsey flinch like a rabbit hearing a condor.

Police radios are the aural equivalent of doctor's handwriting. All of a sudden, the little black metal box goes *squawk-squawk-squawk*, and the cops understand it! Like these two—they understood it when their little metal boxes went *squawk-squawk-squawk*, and this information they'd just received made them relax and even grin at each other. One of them pushed the button on his metal box and told his shoulder, "Ten-four," while the other one handed Rumsey Mr. Jefferson's ID and told him, "Thanks for your cooperation."

Rumsey said, "Huh? Listen, you don't mind, would you tell me? Wha'd they just say there?"

The cops looked surprised. One said, "You didn't hear? They got the guy."

"The one we were looking for," the other one addended.

"Oh," Rumsey said. "Was he me?"

"Move along," said the cop.

Algy came up out of the subway and started walking along the boulevard in the cool October sunshine. Three blocks from the bank he was headed for was another bank, on another corner, this one open for business. As a matter of fact, as Algy walked by its front door, a big-boned guy in a black topcoat, carrying a full grocery store plastic bag, hurtled out of that bank and crashed straight into Algy; this is because the guy wasn't looking where he was going, but leftward, off at traffic along the boulevard.

Neither Algy nor his new dance partner went down, though it looked iffy for a second, and they had to grab at each other's coats. "Easy, big guy," Algy advised, while the guy, increasingly frantic, pulled himself free, waving that plastic bag around over his head, shouting, "Out of the way!"

Algy might have said a cautionary word or two about panic and its discontents, but at that instant a black sedan pulled in by the fire hydrant between them and the curb. The driver, another dark-coated big guy, leaned way over to shove open the passenger door and yell, "Ralph! In!"

Algy stepped back, gesturing for Ralph to go catch his ride, but all at once Ralph had a gun in his hand and a glower on his face and a cluster of Algy's coat sleeve in his fist, as he snarled in Algy's face, "Get in."

Algy couldn't believe it. "Get *in*?"

The driver couldn't believe it, either. "Ralph? What the hell you doin'?"

Over the approaching but still far-off screams of many sirens, under the surveillance of a pair of bank guards, goggle-eyed behind the bank's glass revolving door, Ralph yelled at his partner, "He's a hostage!"

The driver also didn't believe *that*. With one scornful look at Algy, he said, "*He's* no hostage, Ralph. He looks like one of *us*."

"I do, you know," Algy said.

The driver squinted toward his rearview mirror, filling up with nearing patrol cars. "A hostage is a fourteen-year-old girl, Ralph," he explained. "Get in the car."

At last Ralph released Algy's sleeve and jumped into the black sedan, which lunged away into traffic, through the inevitable red light, and on around the corner, with all at once three gumdrops in hot pursuit, and more coming.

One cop car slid to a wheel-locked stop by Algy and the fire hydrant as the two bank guards came running out, both of them pointing at Algy and shouting, "That's one of them!"

"Hey," Algy said.

The two cops got out on both sides of their car to hike up their tool belts and give Algy the fish-eye. "What's your story?" the nearest one wanted to know. His partner was a woman, built low for stability.

"I'm walking by," Algy started.

"They were talking to him," a guard argued.

The woman cop, being the smarter of the pair, pointed at Algy and said to the guards, "Was he in the bank?"

"Well, no," both guards said.

The first cop went back to the first question. "So what *is* your story?"

"I'm walking by," Algy started again, "and the guy come out and run into me, and his car showed up, and he wanted me for a hostage, but the driver said no, a hostage is a fourteen-year-old girl, so they went off to find one."

Wide-eyed, the woman cop said, "They're on their way to kidnap a fourteen-year-old girl?"

Algy shrugged. "I dunno. That's what they said."

The woman cop hopped back into her patrol car to report this development, while her partner abruptly became surrounded by victims from inside the bank, both customers and guards. Over their bobbing heads, the cop called to Algy, "Stick around. You can identify them."

"Sure thing," Algy said, with his most honest smile. Holding the smile, he walked casually backward to the corner and around it, the way, as a kid, he used to sneak into movie houses by looking as though he was coming out. Once away from the sight lines of all that drama, he legged it on out of there.

Big Hooper did not take subways. The cars cramped him, and let's not even talk about the turnstiles. If he had to travel any distance (within the five boroughs, of course—where else is there?), he'd promote the cash he needed one way and another, then phone for a stretch limo, preferably black. The white ones were just a little flashy. He'd take the limo to somewhere near his destination, pay in cash, and if he needed a lift back, he'd call a different service.

Today he'd decided to give the limo driver an address just a few blocks beyond the Sunnyside branch of Immigration Trust, so he could eyeball the place before de-limoing, just in case it might seem like a good idea not to drop in after all.

So they were tooling along eastbound across Queens, maybe a mile, two miles, from their destination, with Big watching a soap opera on the TV in the back of today's (white, what the hell) limo, when it gradually occurred to him that they weren't moving, and they hadn't been moving for quite some little while.

When he looked up from the girl in the hospital bed trying to remember who she was, he saw a lot of stopped cars and the backs of a lot of gawking people. He could tell they were gawking because they kept going up on the balls of their feet, trying to see over the top of one another.

Big offed the TV and said, " 'S it?"

"Some kinda cop thing," the driver said, looking at Big in his interior mirror. He was apparently from some remote, probably mountainous part of Asia that hadn't started outbreeding until very recently. "They got the street closed," he went on.

"Well, take another way," Big told him.

"Can't," the driver said.

"Whadaya mean, can't?"

"Nothing's open." The driver ticked items off on his fingers. "Hunner twenny-third torn up by Brooklyn Gas, shut till Thursday. Prospect closed to ve-*hic*-ular traffic till eleven p.m., block party. Jay blocked by construction until April. Wheeler closed down, a demonstration about charter schools."

Big said, "For or against?"

"Who cares? Then there's Hedlong, they—"

"All right, just a minute," Big said. "Lemme see about this."

He got out of the limo, the driver watching with the look of a man who'd been here in New York City from far-off remotest Asia long enough to know nothing ever helped around here. Regardless, Big walked forward, slicing a V through the gawkers like a bowling ball through lemmings, until he reached the center of attention, beyond a line of blue police sawhorses.

The center of attention, in a cleared semicircle of sidewalk, turned out to be a loony with a knife. Maybe forty years old, in blue and white vertically striped pajamas, ratty maroon bathrobe, barefoot, hair all messed around like a shag rug after a party, unshaved, eyes full of goldfish. He stood with his back against the brick wall of a Neighborhood Clinic, whatever that is, and he kept waving this huge meat cleaver of a knife back and forth, holding off the half-dozen uniformed cops crouched in a crescent in front of him, all of them talking to him, gesturing, explaining, pointing out, none of them holding a gun.

Big knew how that went. Things rode along easy for a while, and whenever the cops met a loony like this on the street—which happens now and again in New York City, though most of them were crazy before they got here—they would just cheerfully blow him away, then explain in the report how the knife or the hammer or the postage meter had seemed at the time to be a serious threat to the officer's life, and that would be that. But then a few incidents would pile up, and the cops would decide to dial down for a while, so, when confronted with a prime prospect for the Off button like this one here, they'd do cajole instead, which never works, but which might possibly keep the loony contained until EMT could get here with the net.

Which hadn't happened yet, and who knew when it would. Big went sideways along this sawhorse to the end, stepped through the gap, and when a lot of cops reached out to restrain him, he said, "Yeah, yeah," shrugged them away, and walked straight to the loony.

The crescent of cops stared at him, not knowing what this was supposed to be. Big ignored them, kept walking toward the loony, stopped well within cleaver range, stuck out his left hand, and said, "Gimme the knife, bozo."

Now, we know this loony really was a loony because, when confronted by Big, he did not immediately say *yessir* and hand over the cutlery. Instead of acting like a sane person, he went on acting like a loony, lunging forward with the cleaver slicing around in a broad sidearm swing, intending to bisect Big at the waist.

The middle of Big's body curved inward as his left hand lifted out of the way of the slashing cleaver, then closed almost gently on the hand behind it. Hand and cleaver stopped as though they'd hit a glass door. With the loony's arm and body still thrusting forward, Big made a quarter turn to his right, like a partner in a very formal dance. His left hand flicked up-down. The crack of the loony's wrist snapping caused a flinch and a queasy look on every cop in the neighborhood.

The cleaver clattered to the ground; so did the loony.

Turning away from his good works, Big nodded at the assembled cops. Before strolling away, "Next time," he advised them, "try a little tenderizing."

Stan was a very law-abiding driver, since the cars he drove invariably belonged to somebody else. For that reason, he obeyed every traffic regulation everywhere, and if he'd had a license, it would have been clean as a whistle. So he was astonished, and not happy, when the county cop on the motorcycle up ahead on the Long Island Expressway suddenly pulled off onto the shoulder, stopped, hopped out of the saddle, and briskly waved Stan down.

No choice—hit the right blinker and pull in behind the bike. He'd always known this moment might someday appear, despite his precautions, and he'd worked out a game plan to deal with it. He intended to claim amnesia and let everybody else sort it out.

But there was something different about this traffic stop. In the first place, the cop, instead of taking that leisurely stroll around to the driver's window that's standard for such encounters, dashed for the passenger door, going *klop-klop* in his high leather boots, face strained with urgency. Yanking open that door, he flung himself backward onto the seat, hurling his left arm out to point, so forcefully he banged his gloved fingertip into the windshield as he cried, "Follow that Taurus!"

Stan looked at him. "What?"

The cop had himself turned around and completely into the car now. As he slammed the door, he aimed a very red face in Stan's direction. "Follow," he said, and thumped his leather-gloved fist on the dashboard, "*that*," and did the fingertip-mash against the windshield again, "TAURUS!"

"Okay, okay."

Stan didn't see any Tauri, but he figured, if he drove the direction the cop kept pointing, sooner or later a Taurus would present itself. It's a popular make of car. So he tromped the accelerator, and the car, a very nice BMW recently in the longterm parking lot at LaGuardia, leaped forward so as to multiple-g the cop backward into his bucket seat.

Taurus, Taurus. The cop peeled himself off the seat to say, "Good, that's good. See him? The green Taurus."

Then Stan did: recent vintage, pallid green, middle lane, moderate speed. "Got him."

"Good. Don't overtake him," the cop warned, "just keep him in sight."

"Piece of cake."

The cop had a little radio high on the angled strap of his Sam Browne belt. Flipping the toggle, he said into it, low but still audible to Stan, "Cycle broke down, commandeered a civilian vehicle, suspects in sight, still eastbound within city limits."

But not for long. Stan watched his exit go by, but he and the Taurus kept heading for Long Island, while the cop's radio made nasal guttural vomiting sounds the cop apparently interpreted as speech, because he said, "Ten-four," which Stan knew cops say because they can never seem to remember "Uh-huh."

Stan had never been commandeered before. He wondered if it came with benefits, but somehow doubted it. He said, "You don't mind my asking, wha'd the Taurus do?"

"Held up a jewelry store in Astoria."

Stan was astonished. "There's jewelry stores in Astoria?"

The cop shrugged. "Why not? Wedding rings, sorry-honeys. Your jewelry store's your universal."

"I suppose you're right," Stan said, and the cop tensed all over, like a sphincter: "He's gonna exit!"

Stan too had seen the Taurus's right directional blink on. Keeping well back, he said, "I suppose these guys are armed and dangerous."

"Jeez, I hope not," the cop said. "I'm on traffic detail. That's why we don't wanna overtake them, make them suspicious, just keep them in sight."

"Ten-four," Stan said.

"When they get stopped at a light," the cop said, "pull up next to them, I'll look it over, see if I can take them down without backup."

Stan knew he was just saying that to cover for what he'd said a minute ago, but what the hell: "You got it."

The cop took off his hat, to be in disguise, and sat forward, eyes tense, licking his lips.

Never had Stan seen anybody so lucky with traffic lights. The Taurus went this way and that way on the city streets, block after block with a traffic light hanging over every intersection, the Taurus steadily trending south by east, and every last one of those traffic lights was green when the Taurus arrived. Sometimes, particularly twice when the Taurus had made a turn at an intersection, Stan had to goose it to scoot through on the yellow, but he figured, he was under cop's orders here; he should be covered.

It bothered him a while, knowing he was part of messing up the day of a couple of fellow mechanics, but then it didn't bother him any more.

Meanwhile, the cop kept talking to his radio, giving it coordinates, progress reports, and the radio kept barfing back. Then the cop tensed again, putting on his hat as he said. "This is it. Next intersection—there!"

They were almost a full block back, a tan Jeep Cherokee between them, the green Taurus almost to the corner, when all at once cop cars came out of everywhere, left and right and practically dropping down from overhead, surrounding the Taurus, blocking it in good and, by the way, freaking out the driver of the Cherokee no end.

Stan slammed on the brakes. "Now what?"

"Wait here!" the cop barked, and jumped from the car.

Fat chance. The Taurus is a very popular car, and wishy-washy green for some reason is a very popular color. One of those moments when the cop had been busy giving coordinates and looking for street signs, Stan had managed to stop following green

Taurus number one and start following green Taurus number two. Therefore, he was already backing to the corner, swinging around it, flooring that BMW out of there, even before the four little old ladies with the missals in their hands came stumbling out of their Taurus to stare at all that firepower.

What with one thing and another, Algy was the first to arrive at the Sunnyside branch of Immigration Trust. At first, he just walked past it, hands in his pockets, looking it over, trusting that nobody with a plastic bag full of loot would come hurtling out of *this* place.

The car had been extracted and taken away. Guys in mustaches and blue jeans and tool belts were slowly closing the facade with sheets of plywood. Streamers of yellow Crime Scene tape were wrapped around everything in sight as though the Easter bunny had been here, bored, nothing else to do in October. And speaking of bored, that's what the two cops were in the prowl car parked out front, the only official presence still here.

The bank was at the corner of a two-story tan-brick structure that ran the length of the block, shops downstairs—Chinese takeout, video rental, dry cleaner, OTB—and apartments above, most of them with window air conditioner rumps mooning the traffic on the boulevard beyond the skimpy plane trees. Each apartment facade was as individual as each store, one bearing RENT STRIKE! signs, one suggesting COME TO JESUS!, one with windows painted black, one crying REMEMBER K   with the rest of the paper torn off, one with what appeared to be curtains *and* blinds *and* drapes. The corner apartment, above the bank, expressed its individuality through paranoia; every window was as barred and gated as a maximum-security cell, and through those iron braces could be read NO TRESPASSING and BEWARE OF DOG and NO SOLICITING and KEEP OUT and PRIVATE PROPERTY.

Downstairs, the bank had been a bit less prepared for intruders. It had been a retail store until its makeover into a branch bank—probably ladies' better fashions—and still retained the large windows along both front and side streets for the display of the merchant's wares; or at least had still retained them until Morry Calhoun had swung by.

The video rental shop was next door to the bank; go in through there? But the shop was open and staffed, and its entrance was very much in the bored cops' sight line.

Algy walked around the corner, to the side street where the bank's former glass had already been replaced by plywood, and at the rear of the building was a solid fence of unpainted vertical wood slats, eight feet high and six feet wide. Approaching it, Algy saw that half its width was a wood-slat door, inset into the fence, with a round metal keyhole but no handle. Behind it, from what he could see over the top of the fence, was an areaway running the length of the block. At this end, it was between the rear of the bank and the blank brick side of the nursing home that fronted on the cross street. And above, a row of fire escapes.

Hmmm. Algy strolled on down the block, crossed the street at the corner, and strolled back again, getting a good look at the rear of the bank building, the fire escapes, the windows of the second-floor apartment, which continued the theme stated along front and side, barred gates, though without the warning notices. The interior behind those windows was dark.

Why not? the first step was to get inside the building, so why not into the apartment above the bank? From there, maybe Morry Calhoun had loosened some structural stuff, and an agile person could come down through the ceiling. Or there'd be a staircase, so the tenant could put trash in the areaway. Or whatever.

Algy next strolled all around the block, away from the bank, pausing on the next cross street over to sit briefly on a fire hydrant while he removed his left shoe, took a few flat flexible pieces of metal from inside the heel, put the shoe back on and resumed his walk.

Nearing the bank again, he held the flexible metal strips

tucked into both palms and zeroed in on that wooden door in the wooden wall. He'd seen that kind of lock before; they were old friends, and this one didn't detain him long.

Inside, as he'd expected, the concrete-floored areaway was garbage-can-strewn. There were doors spaced along the rear wall, but it looked as though the near ones were simply ground-floor access.

On the third leap, he hooked a hand over the bottom rung of the fire escape, which his weight then brought downward, making it easier to climb. At the top, the flexible metal strips worked very nicely to unlock the gate over the nearest window, then slip through between upper and lower sashes of the window itself to gently elbow the window lock out of the way. Slowly, silently, he lifted the window, leaned close to the opening, listened.

Nothing. No TV, no snoring, no whistling teakettle.

Algy slid over the sill, paused to close the gate and window behind himself, then looked around at a small, spartan bedroom. Framed photos of old-time boxers in manly stances were on the walls.

Algy started across the bedroom toward the doorway, and was nearly there when he became aware of the eyes. They were in the hall beyond the bedroom door, they were at crotch height, and they were connected to the largest, meanest-looking, scariest dog Algy had ever seen.

He stopped. The instant he did, the dog started. It didn't bark, because it was more serious than that. It didn't want to make a fuss; it merely wanted to kill Algy, slowly, with its teeth.

Algy turned. Window closed and barred. No time.

A shut door was to his right. He leaped to it, yanked it open, saw clothes hanging on a bar, lunged in among them, pulled the door shut; the dog thudded like a locomotive against the door.

Now what?

*   *   *

John Rumsey's flexible metal tools were just as efficacious as Algy's on that wooden door, but then Rumsey chose to climb the inside of the fence, finding hand and footholds on the angle irons that held fence to building, and so reach the fire escape's upper landing that way. (He was too short to have caught the fire escape by jumping.) He was surprised, at the top, to find that both gate and window were unlocked though shut, but he thought this meant merely that even someone as security-conscious as this tenant appeared to be might eventually grow a little slack. He entered noiselessly, shut gate and window and started across the room, getting just about as far as Algy had before making that same dreadful discovery.

Rumsey wasn't quite as fast as his friend had been. He made it into the closet, but left behind a triangle of trouser leg clenched between the dog's teeth.

Slamming the door, hearing the dog slam into it from the other side, Rumsey became horribly aware that he wasn't alone in here. Someone—or something—rustled and slurfed right next to him. "What?" he called. *Wham*, went the dog against the door.

"I'm not here!" cried a voice. "I can explain!"

A familiar voice. Hardly believing it, Rumsey said, "Algy?"

A little pause. "John?"

Wham, went the dog.

Stan, being a driver, took a slightly different approach. That is, he looked for a means of access that would, in its early phases, include a car. He drove around the block, noted the storefronts, the varied second-floor window treatments, the workmen applying plywood, the bored cops in their cruiser, then the nursing home (barely glancing at the wooden door in the wooden fence); on around the block, coming up at last to the far end of the building holding the bank.

On this block, the space equivalent to the nursing home at the other end was occupied by an open-sided four-story parking garage. Stan made note of that, turned at the corner, drove on down past the cops and the bank and the workmen, took that next turn, and pulled to a stop just short of the wooden fence.

Plywood now covered the former windows on the side of the bank, but the blue police sawhorses were still there, swathed in gay yellow Crime Scene tape. Stan got out of the BMW, opened the trunk, and leaned in to open the small pass-through door between trunk and backseat, placed there because the kind of people who own this kind of car usually also own skis.

The sawhorses came in three parts: two A-shaped sets of legs and the ten-foot-long crossbar, a two-by-six plank. Stan rescued two of these planks from their legs and the yellow tape and wrestled them into the BMW, having to fold the front passenger seat down as well to ootch them in all the way. Then he drove around the block again, turned in at the parking garage, and took his ticket from the machine.

He found a useful parking slot on the sloping third level, backed into it so the rear of the BMW was close to the waist-high concrete-block barrier that was all the building had for exterior walls, and slid the sawhorse planks out of the car and across the intervening space between parking garage and bank building roof, though down the block from the bank, closer to the middle of the building. The planks fit very nicely, with good overhang at each end. Stan went across on all fours—two per plank—then walked briskly along the roof to the final fire escape. He went down that, found the unlocked window, climbed in, saw the dog, the dog saw him, Stan bolted for the closet, and soon another reunion took place, though not an entirely happy one.

Big knew he was a memorable guy, and so shouldn't walk past those cops in the cruiser, no matter how bored they were, more than once. He strolled down the block, took in the scene, turned down the side street, saw a couple of blue sawhorse leg sets lying on the sidewalk, remarked to himself that cops were usually neater than that, and noticed that where the next to last sheet of plywood overlapped the last sheet of plywood, there was a bit of a gap where the plywood might have been screwed down a bit more securely but was not.

With a quick glance around to note that he was alone out here, he stepped to the plywood, inserted a hand in the space, and tugged. He had to tug three times, finally, and then be a little careful of jutting screws, but with a small pivot like the hippopotami in *Fantasia* he curled around the opening he'd made, and entered the bank. Two tugs were sufficient to pull the plywood back to its original position, or at least to look as though it were in its original position, and then Big went for a stroll through the empty, and rather messy, bank.

Morry Calhoun and his Infiniti had done a pretty complete job in here. He'd come angling through the plate glass, so that just by showing up he'd pretty well cleared out the front of the place, but then the Infiniti had also hit a couple of tables where people could fill out deposit slips and the like, and bounced them deeper into the bank, which is what took out the side windows as well as parts of the tellers' cages and all the frosted glass fronting the loan officer's separate cubicle. Shards of glass, slivers of wood, pens with chains attached, wheeled swivel chairs and wrinkled loan applications were scattered everywhere, all of it a bit hard to see, since Morry and his car had also taken out the electricity.

Big picked his way through the debris to the tellers' cages, where unfortunately there was no cash, since the bank had been closed when Morry arrived and all the money was in the vault for the night. The vault, when Big reached it, was undented but also unopened. It had a time lock, which Big had been hoping for, but with the electricity out, the vault thought it was still one-thirty in the morning, so forget that.

It was just too hard to see in here. Would the branch manager have a flashlight in his office? Why not?

The manager's office had also, at one time, been sheathed in frosted glass, which now went *crunch-crunch* beneath Big's feet. He opened desk drawers, pawed around, and in the bottom right found a small flashlight with a dying battery. By its dim light he saw there was nothing else of interest in the desk, but what was that underneath it?

The night deposit box. Morry's Infiniti had drop-kicked it across the bank, through the frosted glass, and into the manager's office, where it had come to rest partially under the desk.

And totally cracked open. In the flashlight's wan beam, Big saw the thick envelopes inside that metal box with the twisted-open door, and when he withdrew the envelopes every one of them was full of money. Only some of the money was cash, the rest being checks or travelers' checks or credit card slips (all of which Big left behind), but the cash was a nice amount, enough to make him look around the office for something to carry it all in.

And what have we here? A gray canvas bag, about a foot long and four inches deep, with a lockable zippered top. An actual money bag—what better for carrying money? Big filled it with the cash from the night deposit, then filled his pockets with the leftover, then decided to leave.

But. As he came out of the office, the flashlight weakly glimmering its last in his fist, he heard a sudden nasty whirring sound. It seemed to come from where he'd made entry, between the plywoods.

Yes. Apparently, the workmen were just about finished, and in making one last double-check of their work they'd noticed the same inefficient gap that had drawn Big's attention, which they were now correcting, with another complete sheet of plywood. The whirring sounds were their portable drills, and every whirr produced another screw spinning through sheets of plywood and into the bank, a full inch of leftover screw sticking through plywood every foot or so all around this area.

Never get through that. Big didn't like the concept of being able to get in without being able to get out, but this was looking very much like the concept he'd been dealt.

The whirring stopped. The workmen were gone. Outside, it was still a bright and sunny fall morning, while inside, in the dying of the light, Big paced the perimeter of his prison, looking for a way out.

When he reached the front of the bank, where the entrance door used to be, he looked up, and the ceiling looked funny. *Damn* this flashlight. But wasn't that a gap up there, between ceiling and wall?

What this required was to move a desk under that bit of ceiling, then put a second desk on top of it, then carry a chair—non-wheeled, non-swivel—up onto the top of the second desk, climb from desk to desk to chair, and there it was.

At this spot, directly above the original point of impact, the front wall had sagged down away from the ceiling, pulling a piece of ceiling after it. Big could reach that Sheetrock ceiling from here, and when he tugged, a big, irregular chunk of it fell away, missed him, hit both desks, and smacked onto the floor.

What was above? A two-by-six beam, also sagging down at this end, since the wall it had always been attached to wasn't in the right place any more. Big tugged tentatively at the beam, not wanting the whole place to come crashing down on him, and the beam moved in a spongy way, still firmly attached at other spots along its length but willing to angle down now if Big insisted.

He did. The floorboards above the beam popped free, not wanting to come down, but then, they would push *up*. And now Big needed more height.

The loan officer's four-drawer filing cabinet. He pulled out the drawers, dragged the cabinet to his desk-and-chair construction, lifted it up onto the second desk, then put the chair on top of the cabinet, climbed the open front of the cabinet, where the drawers used to be, climbed the chair, pushed some floorboards and some rug out of the way, then tossed the money bag up there. When it didn't come back, he used the dangling beam and the front wall of the building for leverage and worked his way up through ceiling/floor into a small, austere living room with not much more than a narrow sofa, a small TV and reproductions of race horse paintings on the walls.

A back way out. Big picked up the money bag, walked through the apartment to the bedroom, and there he saw a big, ugly dog seated in front of a closed closet door. The dog saw Big, curled his upper lip back over his teeth, turned and hurled himself at Big, who sidestepped, grabbed the hurtling dog by the throat, spun him around, opened the closet door, tossed the dog in, shut the door.

He was just turning toward the rear windows when pandemonium started in the closet: yelling, screaming, crashing around. Now what?

Big turned back to frown at the door, against which there was now a staccato rat-a-tat of frenzied knocking—wasn't there a handle on the inside? Apparently not, since muffled voices— more than one?—hoarsely begged from in there, "Lemme *out!*"

It was curiosity that made Big go back to reopen that door, and out tumbled three men and a dog. "Not you again," Big said, grabbed the dog in the same throat hold as before, and tossed him back onto the pile of clothing now messed up on the closet floor instead of lined up neatly on hangers. Slamming the door yet again, he turned to the three men on the floor, flopping around down there like caught fish in a bucket, and said, "And what the hell is all this?"

Rumsey blinked like an owl in the wrong barn. Around him, everybody was in confused, chaotic motion. On his right, "I can explain!" Algy yelled, while on his left, "Who are you people?" Stan demanded.

Rumsey gazed upward. "Big?" He withdrew Algy's elbow

from his right eye, Stan's knee from his solar plexus. *"Big?"* It was like a dream. A very strange dream.

The big man who'd rescued them, whether he wanted to or not, looked around at the three doing their Raggedy Andys on the floor. "I know you birds," he said.

"Of course you do," Stan said, having recovered his memory.

Rumsey, climbing up Algy to get to his feet, said, "I saw this thing in the *News* about Morry Calhoun—"

Stan, climbing up the bed to get to his feet, said, "—great shot of the car in the bank—"

Algy, scrambling around on the floor until Big grabbed him by the scruff of the neck and set him upright, said, "—so I thought I'd come see, is there any spillage."

"There was some," Big told him. "Not much." He gestured at the gray canvas money bag on the bed.

They all looked at it. Unfortunately, they understood, that bag belonged to Big now.

Rumsey spoke for them all—except Big—when he said, "All this, for nothing."

"I got mine, anyway," Big said comfortably. "I always get mine."

Algy said to the others, "And Big did come in handy with the dog, you got to admit."

"And I got wheels," Stan told them, "anybody wants a lift anywhere."

Rumsey was not consoled. He said, "What I come out here for wasn't wheels, or to get saved from some dog. What I come out here for was a score."

"Well, you know," Algy said, "I happen to be aware"—he looked at his watch—"twenty minutes ago, a bank three blocks from here was knocked over by a couple not very skillful guys. They didn't get much."

Rumsey said, "I don't have to hear about other guys' scores, not even little ones."

"The point I'm making here," Algy said, "is twenty minutes ago. The plainclothes detectives didn't get there yet. You know, the victim interviews."

Rumsey's head and eyes and spirits lifted. "Everybody's rattled," he said. "They've shut the bank, but they're still there."

Stan said, "The security tape's been taken away for evidence."

Algy whipped a hand into and out of his trouser pocket, flashed at them a gold badge in a brown leather case, pocketed it again, said, "I always carry a little ID. You never know."

Big said, "Algy? What if a cop frisks you one time, takes a look at that?"

Algy grinned at him. "It says, 'Love Detective, Licensed To Kiss.'"

Rumsey segued into a look that was very caring, very concerned, very earnest. In a voice like a funeral director, he said, "Mr. Manager, are you *certain* those felons didn't gain access to your vault? We'd better check that out."

Big laughed. "Nice to run into you fellas," he said.

Ten minutes after the apartment was empty, the dog finally started howling, but there was nobody around to listen.

CODA

When the vault door was at last reopened at three-thirty that afternoon to release the imprisoned bank employees, one of them, Rufold Hepple, had to be carried out by five fellow tellers, one at each limb and one at his head. (Fortunately, he was a skinny little fellow and didn't weigh much.) "I'll be all right," he kept telling everybody who looked down at him. "Just as soon as I get home, I'll be fine."

There were white-clad ambulance attendants in among the blue police officers and black-and-yellow firefighters, and they kept asking him, as he lay supine on the faux marble floor, head cushioned by several empty money sacks, if he didn't want to go to the hospital, be looked at, checked over; but his fears of (a) hospitals, (b) doctors, and (c) people dressed completely in white, kept him saying over and over, "No, I'll be fine; I'll be fine. Get my strength back in a minute. I'll be fine as soon as I get home."

The nearly four hours in the pitch-black vault had been the worst experience of Rufold Hepple's life, calling into play simultaneously so many of his deep-seated fears, it was as though he'd been strapped into one of those machines for mixing paint. There was his fear of darkness, for instance, and his fear of crowds, his fear of unusual smells (several of his coworkers, when confined for a long time in a small, dark space, had turned out to have very unusual smells indeed), his fear of small, confined spaces. (It was his fear of long words derived from the Greek that kept him from even *thinking* the proper medical terms for all these fears.)

Lying there on the floor, with only his fear of being noticed by other people still actively searing him, Rufold Hepple continued to give himself, as he had in the vault, the courage to survive this ordeal, by thinking only of his own little home, so near, so soon to protect him again. It was the great paradox of his life that only the comfort and security of his very own little apartment gave him the strength necessary to leave it every day, for his job here at the bank, or to shop, or to make his twice-weekly visits to Dr. Bananen, just around the corner.

In just a few minutes now, he would be ready. He would stand, smile, show them all nothing, leave the bank, march the three blocks home and up the stairs and through the many locks, to be greeted by his only friend, his dear dog Sigmund. In just a few minutes. Just a few minutes, and he would be safe and sound.

31901063555173

CPSIA information can be obtained
at www.ICGtesting.com
Printed in the USA
FFHW02n0809270818
48035283-51748FF